ABBY'S UN-VALENTINE

**Other books by
Ann M. Martin**

P.S. Longer Letter Later
(written with Paula Danziger)
Leo the Magnificat
Rachel Parker, Kindergarten Show-off
Eleven Kids, One Summer
Ma and Pa Dracula
Yours Turly, Shirley
Ten Kids, No Pets
Slam Book
Just a Summer Romance
Missing Since Monday
With You and Without You
Me and Katie (the Pest)
Stage Fright
Inside Out
Bummer Summer

THE KIDS IN MS. COLMAN'S CLASS series
BABY-SITTERS LITTLE SISTER series
THE BABY-SITTERS CLUB mysteries
THE BABY-SITTERS CLUB series
CALIFORNIA DIARIES series

ABBY'S UN-VALENTINE

Ann M. Martin

AN
APPLE
PAPERBACK

SCHOLASTIC INC.
New York Toronto London Auckland Sydney
Mexico City New Delhi Hong Kong

Cover art by Hodges Soileau

No part of this publication may be reproduced in whole or in part, or stored in a retrieval system, or transmitted in any form or by any means, electronic, mechanical, photocopying, recording, or otherwise, without written permission of the publisher. For information regarding permission, write to Scholastic Inc., Attention: Permissions Department, 555 Broadway, New York, NY 10012.

ISBN 0-590-50350-2

12 11 10 9 8 7 6 5 4 3 2   9/9 0 1 2 3 4/0

Printed in the U.S.A.   40
First Scholastic printing, January 1999

The author gratefully acknowledges
Nola Thacker
for her help in
preparing this manuscript.

ABBY'S UN-VALENTINE

CHAPTER 1

If everyone is going to make such a big deal out of Valentine's Day, then why isn't it a real holiday? Why don't we have the day off? Why do we have to go to school? You want to show some real heart, close school for the day.

When Kristy Thomas, our fearless leader and president of the Baby-sitters Club (also known as the BSC — more about that later), runs for President of the United States, I'm going to suggest that as one of the planks in her platform.

As it is, Valentine's Day is just an excuse for candy and universal silliness. The candy I don't mind, but the silliness I could live without. When I realized February 14th was almost upon us, I hoped Stoneybrook Middle School, or SMS, would not descend into valentine madness the way my school on Long Island did. But I quickly learned that the red-heart syndrome infested Connecticut as well as New

1

York. At least two weeks before the date, the memos on the bulletin board next to the principal's office appeared on red paper (including a memo about the school's Valentine Day's Dance, on red paper cut into a heart shape, in case we missed the point). Teachers began to decorate their classrooms with paper heart chains strung from one end of the room to the other. Really fanatic teachers even taught about Valentine's Day. Dolly One (one of two teachers at SMS with more than a passing resemblance to Dolly Parton), also known as Mrs. Bernhardt, my history teacher, gave us a little lesson on Saint Valentine, who may or may not have been a mythical figure.

Mythical or not, he clearly had some influence in Stoneybrook. I briefly considered volunteering to do an extra-credit report for Dolly One, exploding the whole Valentine's Day myth and revealing it for the overly sentimental, overly celebrated advertising campaign that it really is.

But who wants to be a Valentine Scrooge? Not even I, Abigail Stevenson of Stoneybrook, Connecticut.

So I kept quiet and tried not to remember my unhappy history with V-day — like the year, back on Long Island, I decided not to waste my time sending valentines to my friends. We used to stick Valentine's Day cards through the vents in our lockers, which most people at our school decorated for the big day, turning them into big valentine mailboxes. I opened my locker at the end of the day and found it full of valentines. I felt really crummy and totally embarrassed.

And then there was the time, when I was much, much younger, when Anna, my twin sister, and I bought a box of valentine candy for Mom and Dad. It was my favorite kind of chocolate candy. I loved the heart-shaped box, and I kept opening it to stare at the chocolates. Then I took just one chocolate. And then another.

You know what happened next, don't you? You're right. I ate the whole box.

Mom and Dad found out because by dinner that night I had a major stomachache. They thought it was pretty funny. My father said, "Abby, next time save a little to share with the rest of us." But Anna was furious with me for weeks, even when I paid back her half of the money we'd used to buy the candy. And let her have the heart-shaped box.

That kind of candy, in a heart-shaped box, is still my favorite.

And then there was the V-day in fifth grade, when Perk Watkins decided he wanted me to be his valentine. He followed me around, gave me a bag of those little candy hearts with sayings like "Be Mine" and "Forever Yours" printed on them, and made me the laughing-stock of the whole school. Fortunately, I came down with a bad cold and had to stay home for a week. When I went back, Perk had transferred his attentions to someone else.

So you can see that Valentine's Day and I are not made for each other. I do not want a BF (boyfriend). I do not want to play kissyface in the halls the way some people do. Although some people (Mary Anne Spier, the secretary of the BSC, for instance) are dating genuinely nice, mature guys who don't say gross or stupid things and are fun to hang around with, I have noticed that most guys my age are, well, a little immature. So, while BFs are fine in theory — especially if, like Mary Anne and her BF, Logan, you truly enjoy each other's company — I've decided to wait on the whole deal, to give the guys a chance to grow up a little.

Meanwhile, I have plenty to do. I have athletics, including soccer, only the most perfect sport in the world (INVENTED BY MEN, PERFECTED BY WOMEN, as one of my favorite T-shirts says). I am a member of the aforementioned Baby-sitters Club, which means I do a lot of baby-sitting. I have schoolwork, which, since I am an average student, keeps me on my toes. And, of course, I have my family and my allergies and my asthma.

Allergies? Asthma? How can such things keep you busy? Easy, when life makes you sneeze. I travel with an inhaler in case I have an asthma attack. And I have to be careful because a bad attack could send me to the hospital (it's happened a couple of times). I'm planning on outgrowing all this, but meanwhile I am allergic to cat litter, milk, shellfish, and probably dozens of things I don't even know about yet. Which brings us back to February and V-day. The one good thing about the day is that it falls during a month when pollen doesn't plug the air, when the pollution count is generally low, and when the things that make me sneeze do not rule (at least, not so much). It means that I can wear my contacts instead of my glasses because I don't have to deal with watery eyes. It means that I can smell things (chocolate, not flowers).

So as long as no one sends me any valentine flowers, I'm willing to admit that the day has a good point.

I was thinking about all these things as I slammed my locker at the end of that Wednesday, not quite two weeks before V-day, and paused to admire its un-valentine decorated surface.

"A penny for your thoughts," said a vaguely familiar voice. I looked up to see Ross Brown, who has a locker at the other end of the hall.

"Prices have gone up," I joked. "Didn't you know that? I charge a lot more for my thoughts."

Ross laughed.

I smiled. Not everyone appreciates my sense of humor.

"Hey, Ross. Hi, Abby," said Claudia Kishi, approaching us with her best friend, Stacey McGill.

"Hi," Ross said. To me he said, "See you later, Abby. And next time, I'll be sure to make you an offer you can't refuse."

I laughed.

"Huh?" said Claudia.

"Just a dumb joke," I explained. "What's up?"

"We're going over to Claud's to do homework before the BSC meeting," Stacey said. "Want to come?"

I thought about it. I remembered the gruesome math homework with which we'd been presented earlier, remembered also that Stacey is a math whiz, and said, "Sure."

"You can call your mom from my room," Claudia offered. Claudia is the vice-president of the BSC. She has her own phone line, which is the reason the BSC meets in her room. But I'll explain all the details in a little while.

"I can tell Anna," I said. "She has orchestra practice. We can stop by on our way out."

So we did. Anna was doing something to the bow of her violin when I waved to her from the door of the practice room. Anna and I are identical twins (I am eight minutes younger than she is). We both have pointed faces; curly, dark brown hair (Anna wears hers a little shorter than mine, but not much); the same deep brown eyes; and even the same way of talking. Besides Anna's slightly shorter hair, the only other outward difference is that Anna wears her glasses more often than I do. Of course, we differ in plenty of other ways too. Anna's musical, and I can't carry a tune in a bucket. Anna has a case of scoliosis and has to wear a brace to correct the curve of her spine. (You can't really tell). Anna's not allergic to anything — except sports. (Her idea of athletic endeavor is to wish me luck before a soccer game.) I joined the BSC and Anna didn't, because she wanted to concentrate on her music. Those are just a few of the ways you could tell us apart.

But side by side, we look pretty, well, identical. In fact, we used to get a big kick out of switching with each other when we were kids. And, needless to say, one of our favorite videos is the old Disney movie with Hayley Mills *The Parent Trap*, about twins who switch places.

I told Anna my big plans for the afternoon and she nodded. "I'll be home before Mom, so I'll let her know," she said.

"Thanks," I replied. I looked around at all the musical instruments and added, "Have a good workout."

Anna grinned. "You mean practice? Thanks."

I grinned back. "Whatever."

I waved and left. Anna doesn't always appreciate my sense of humor, even though we are twins. But it's nice when she does.

Of course, Anna *loves* V-day.

But then, nobody's perfect . . . not even my twin sister.

CHAPTER 2

The first thing Claudia said when Mary Anne walked into the meeting at 5:26 that afternoon was, "Has Logan asked you to the Valentine's Day Dance yet?"

Claudia, Stacey, and I had just finished putting away our homework, and Claudia was shifting into her catering mode. By this I mean she was opening drawers, peering behind the headboard of her bed, and excavating secret stashes of junk food from other places around her room. Claudia is a junk food fanatic, something her parents unfortunately don't understand. They consider junk food on the level of the Nancy Drew mysteries that Claudia loves to read, so Claudia squirrels books and bags of chocolate away, where her parents won't see them.

As long as Claud eats her vegetables and doesn't pork out, I don't understand what the problem is. But then, Claudia's parents are

9

stricter than my mom. Compared to most parents, my mom gives me a lot of freedom.

That's because Anna and I had to grow up fast four years ago, when our father was killed in a car accident. It happened very suddenly. One morning I had a father and by that afternoon, I didn't. It changed the way I looked at the world. For a long time, I couldn't laugh. I felt that by laughing I might betray him.

It's better now. But I still miss him. We all do.

Anyway, Mom works long hours at her new job at a publishing house in New York City (which is one of the reasons we moved to Stoneybrook — Mom couldn't take the long, long commute on the Long Island Railroad). She trusts Anna and me with a lot more independence than most of the other kids I know who are the same age.

Of course, even without parental influence my junk food intake would be limited to some extent by my allergies. But I had no problem with the salt-and-vinegar chips Claudia tossed in my direction. I began to munch blissfully.

Mary Anne blushed, but she didn't look surprised by Claudia's abrupt greeting. "Yes, Logan's asked me to the dance," she said. "Last night. He called."

Kristy frowned. I sensed that I might have a fellow valentine-phobe. She cleared her throat, looked at Claudia's clock, and sighed.

The clock now read 5:27. I knew the sigh meant Kristy wanted to start the meeting, but she couldn't rag anybody for being late yet. Our meetings don't start until 5:30.

Sharp. By Madame President's decree.

5:28.

Claudia passed a bag of pretzels to Stacey and began distributing Hershey's Kisses wrapped in red foil. She unwrapped a Kiss for herself carefully, saving the foil.

"Art?" I inquired.

5:29.

Kristy straightened in her chair and cleared her throat.

Jessica Ramsey and Shannon Kilbourne came through the door.

"We're heeere," sang Jessi, giving Kristy a great big smile.

I won't say Kristy looked crestfallen, but she did look a little disappointed. She enjoys those occasions when she can exercise her authority.

But she made up for it by the way she rapped out, just as the clock rolled over to 5:30, "This meeting of the BSC will come to order."

"Art," Claudia agreed, nodding at me and taking another Kiss from the bag before passing it to Shannon and Jessi.

Claudia is an artist.

But wait. I guess if I were an artist, you'd find the picture I've made so far pretty confusing. So I'll tell you all you need to know about the BSC, starting with Kristy (that should please her).

But then, the BSC started with Kristy. It was one of her Brilliant Ideas. She was inspired by watching her mother call several baby-sitters one afternoon, trying to find someone to watch Kristy's younger brother, David Michael. What if a person could call one number and reach several baby-sitters at once, Kristy thought.

The next day, she put her thoughts into action, recruiting Mary Anne, her next-door neighbor and best friend, and Claudia, another good friend, who lived across the street. In no time, business was (baby) booming, and the BSC grew and grew. We now have six regular members, plus two associate members and two honorary members. All of us are thirteen and in the eighth grade at SMS except Shannon, who goes to Stoneybrook Day School, a private school, and Mal and Jessi, who are eleven and in sixth grade. Regular members are required to attend every meeting unless prevented by an emergency or a BSC job. Associate members don't have to attend meetings, but they are trusty, tried-and-true backup when we have more work than we can handle. Honorary members are inactive, usually because they've moved away.

We meet Monday, Wednesday, and Friday afternoons, from five-thirty until six at Claudia's. Clients know that if they call us during meeting times, they'll reach six reliable, experienced baby-sitters. Since Claudia has her own phone number, the line isn't busy with family calls (and Claud's family isn't prevented from using the phone while we are meeting). When a client calls, Mary Anne checks the record book to see who is available and we schedule the baby-sitting appointment.

We pay dues every Monday. The club uses the money to pay Kristy's older brother Charlie for gas (he usually drives Kristy and me to meetings — I live two houses down the street from Kristy), to contribute to Claudia's refreshments fund, to splurge on the occasional pizza party, and to keep our Kid-Kits stocked.

Kid-Kits are another Kristy invention. Every club member has one: a box decorated according to our individual style (my latest Kid-Kit is an old soccer shoe box, with the picture of the soccer shoes outlined in glitter). We fill the boxes with games, toys, books, puzzles (new and hand-me-down), stickers, crayons, and anything else we think might interest a cranky, bored, or shy baby-sitting charge. Our Kid-Kits don't go along on every job. We use them as secret weapons when kids might have cabin fever from being stuck inside by the weather or a bad cold, or to win the trust of a new kid when we sit for new clients.

The record book is Mary Anne's responsibility as club secretary. In it, she writes down all our baby-sitting appointments, our other appointments (such as Jessi's dance classes), and all the pertinent information about our clients — names, addresses, rates paid, and important details: who is allergic to milk, for example, or who might have developed a phobia about cats. Amazingly, Mary Anne has never, ever made a mistake in that record book.

Kristy also instituted the BSC notebook, in which we keep an ongoing journal of our jobs. It's a pain to write up what happened on each job, but it's fun to read — and useful. The past experiences of other members can be very helpful in solving problems when they arise.

Kristy is the president of the BSC not only because she came up with the idea, but also because she likes to be in charge of things. She is extremely organized and very opinionated. With Kristy, the main rule is that things are done her way. It is often difficult (although not *quite* impossible) to convince her to change her mind.

Like me, Kristy had to do some fast growing up, not because her father died, but because he walked out one day when David Michael was a baby. That left Kristy, David Michael, who is seven now, Sam (now fourteen) and Charlie (now sixteen) (their two older brothers) and Kristy's mom on their own.

It wasn't easy. They all had to work hard, and the kids took on a lot of responsibility. But they managed it. Then, in a fairy-tale-like moment, Kristy's mom fell in love with Watson Brewer. I don't know if Watson qualifies as a prince among men, but he turned out to be very nice, *and* a millionaire. When he and Kristy's mom got married, the Thomases moved to the Brewer mansion across town.

Now Kristy is a member of a very large blended family. Fortunately, the mansion is large enough to hold everybody. "Everybody" includes Kristy; her brothers and mother and Watson; Watson's two kids from his first marriage, Karen, who is seven, and Andrew, four, every other month; Emily Michelle, who is two and a half and who Kristy's family adopted from Vietnam; Nannie, Kristy's maternal grandmother, who joined the family to help keep things running smoothly; a Bernese mountain dog puppy named Shannon; a guide-dog-in-training puppy named Scout; a new kitten named Pumpkin (their cranky old cat, Boo-Boo, recently went to the Great Mouse Hunting Grounds in the Sky); and even, according to Karen (who has a vivid imagination), the ghost of Ben Brewer, one of Watson's ancestors.

Naturally, Kristy has to speak loudly and firmly to make herself heard. Some people think she is bossy, but I suspect they are the disorganized people of the world, who don't know how to get things done. She *is* stubborn, though. She even argues with *me*!

It may be that Kristy has another reason for speaking up: She is the shortest person in our class. Kristy has brown hair, medium-fair skin, and big brown eyes. She usually wears what we call her uniform: jeans, a sweatshirt or pullover sweater, and running shoes. Her clothes are about comfort, not style. She doesn't want to waste her time on things she considers frivolous. Kristy is a decent student and one of those people who aren't just sports fans but sports fanatics (one of her best qualities, in my opinion).

Mary Anne, who is Kristy's best friend, has known Kristy since they were babies. Maybe that is why they are best friends, or maybe it really is true that opposites attract, because two people couldn't be more different. Mary Anne is shy and sensitive. Her feelings are easily hurt and her brown eyes have been known to fill with tears at sentimental TV commercials. Like Kristy, Mary Anne is short (she's the second-shortest person in our grade) and lives in a blended family, but the family is much smaller. Plus, Mary Anne started out as an only child — and half an orphan.

That's because Mary Anne's mother died when Mary Anne was just a baby and too young to remember her. Mr. Spier raised Mary Anne on his own. He was very, very strict, because he didn't want to make any mistakes. I was amazed when I heard about all the rules that Mary Anne had to follow. Until recently, her father even picked out her clothes and made her wear her hair in little-kid braids.

Fortunately, Mary Anne was able to convince Mr. Spier that she was growing up and could take more responsibility for herself. Now she picks out her own clothes (casually preppy), wears her brown hair cut short, and has a kitten named Tigger. She was even the first among the BSC members to have a steady boyfriend.

Mr. Spier loosened up even more after he got married again — to his old high school sweetheart, Sharon Schafer, who had moved back to Stoneybrook from California after she and her husband got divorced.

With Mrs. Schafer came her daughter, Dawn, and her son, Jeff. Dawn and Mary Anne became best friends before they were sisters. After the wedding, Mary Anne and Mr. Spier moved into the Schafer house on Burnt Hill

Road, which has an old barn and even a secret passage that was once used by the Underground Railroad.

Dawn was — I mean, is — tall and thin, with white-blonde hair, a few freckles on her tanned nose (Mary Anne has skin that tans but doesn't freckle), and two earrings in each earlobe. She's a fan of the beach-casual style. Dawn likes to surf and is a health food crusader and a righteous environmentalist. If the kids for whom Dawn baby-sat didn't "reduce, reuse, recycle" when they first met Dawn, they did soon.

The reason I almost referred to Dawn in the past tense is because Dawn doesn't live here anymore. Her brother, Jeff, was unhappy in Connecticut and missed California. Even before the wedding, he decided to go back there and live with his dad. Dawn soon realized that she felt the same way — plus, she missed Jeff — and so, as difficult as it was for her, she also returned to California. She's still an honorary BSC member, and she baby-sits when she's here for visits.

Claudia, as you already know, is vice-president of the BSC, a junk food gourmet, and an artist. She is probably the most striking-looking club member, not only because of her creamy complexion, long shiny black hair, and dark, dark brown eyes, but also because she is her own personal artwork. Claudia doesn't buy clothes, she creates outfits. I always look forward to seeing in what way Claudia will reinvent herself each day.

Today she was dressed in ski-lodge mode. That meant a woolly sweater, long black tights with thick blue socks, and hiking boots. But these weren't just any hiking boots — they were tied with shiny silver shoelaces with little snowflakes on the ends. They'd also been decorated — by Claudia — with a motif of snow-capped mountains running along the outside of each boot.

Claud's sweater was blue, white, and gray with a snowflake-patterned yoke. It was enormous, stretching almost to her knees. Her hair was pulled back in a long braid. From one ear dangled a silver earring in the shape of a pair of crossed skis, and from the other hung a small silver polar bear. This was actually a somewhat conservative fashion statement for Claudia, but you couldn't help noticing how good she made it look.

One day Claudia will be famous for her art, but right now she has to struggle with all the non-art subjects in school. She's smart, but she doesn't see the world in terms of grammar and numbers and historical dates. She sees it in terms of art. That's why she's had to have special tutoring (she even had to make a brief return to seventh grade) and why her parents monitor her schoolwork pretty closely. Matters aren't helped by the fact that Claudia's older sister, Janine, is an official genius who, although only in high school, is taking college courses. (However, she doesn't share Claudia's artistic genius.)

Anastasia McGill (call her Stacey, or else!) is our treasurer, because she is a math whiz, as I mentioned, and a generally good student. She's also the other fashion maven in the BSC, which may be one of the reasons she and Claudia are best friends. Where Claudia's style is a personal artistic statement, Stacey's is more up-to-the-second stylish. It reflects Stacey's sophistication, which sometimes makes her seem a little older than the rest of us.

Stacey, who is an only child, lived in New York before she moved with her parents to Stoneybrook. (Her mother and father are divorced now, and her father has returned to Manhattan, so Stacey visits there often.) Stacey may also seem older than thirteen because of a physical challenge. She has diabetes. When Stacey's parents discovered that, they went into anxious-parent overdrive. Like Mary Anne, Stacey had to work hard to convince her parents that she could be responsible for taking care of herself.

Stacey's diabetes requires close attention, even more than my asthma and allergies.

When a person has diabetes, his or her body doesn't make enough insulin, which helps break down the sugar in foods. So Stacey has to regulate what and when she eats very, very carefully, or she could get very, very sick — maybe even go into a coma. She also has to give herself insulin injections every day.

But as with most things, Stacey stays calmly in control (an excellent quality in a baby-sitter). Even her style projects confidence. For example, today she was wearing a short, dark brown leather skirt over pale stockings. She had on these cool boots that came to just above her knees. Her sweater was the color of butter, and it looked unbelievably soft. There were three pearl buttons at the collar. Stacey had left two of them unbuttoned. Her blonde hair was pulled into a French braid, and she was wearing what looked like real pearl earrings. If there was makeup on her pale, flawless complexion, you couldn't tell.

Jessi, who is our junior officer (which means, because she's only eleven, that she can't baby-sit at night unless it's for her own family), is a ballet dancer. She takes special lessons at Stamford Ballet School every week and has already danced some important roles — Clara in *The Nutcracker*, for example. Her style reflects her passion for dance. She often wears leotards under her sweaters — sometimes with matching tights — and she sometimes goes bunhead, pulling her black hair into a bun on the back of the head, the way ballet dancers do. She favors pastel colors that complement her medium-brown skin and dark brown eyes. She has been known to do dance stretches at BSC meetings.

When I think of dedication and self-discipline, I think of Jessi. She gets up *every* morning at 5:29 to practice her ballet movements at the *barre* her family built for her in the basement. On those mornings when I have trouble psyching myself up for a practice run, I think of Jessi at her *barre* and that rolls me right out of bed! (And yes, I've done my share of stretches at BSC meetings too. In fact, Jessi has taught me a few.)

Like Stacey and me, Jessi moved to Stoney-brook not long ago. She and her mother; father; sister, Becca; and baby brother, John Philip Ramsey, Jr., also known as Squirt, came here from New Jersey. Jessi and Mallory Pike, who was our other junior officer, became best friends after they discovered a mutual love of horses, horse stories, and mysteries.

Mallory, however, is no longer with us. She's now an honorary member, like Dawn. That's because she's gone to boarding school. We're all waiting to hear what she thinks of it. And, of course, we miss her. As the oldest sibling of eight, including a set of triplets, Mallory

22

brought a lifetime of training to the job of baby-sitting and she was excellent at it. She was also a great storyteller, which explains why her ambition is to be a children's book writer and illustrator someday.

Mallory's absence explains Shannon's presence. Without Mallory, we need some temporary help and Shannon, as an associate member, is taking turns with our other associate member, Logan, at filling in the gap and attending some of the meetings.

Shannon, as I mentioned, goes to Stoneybrook Day School (uniforms required!). She's a neighbor of mine — and Kristy's. She and Kristy got off to a, well, contentious beginning when they met. Maybe one reason they did is because they have more than a few things in common, such as world-class organizational skills and a lot of ambition.

Shannon, however, channels her energies into school, maybe more than any of the rest of us. She is a member of the debate team and the Honor Society. She takes philosophy and psychology classes and is the only eighth-grader in the Astronomy Club, of which she is vice-president. And when the Drama Club put on *Arsenic and Old Lace*, Shannon had one of the leads.

Shannon wasn't in uniform at the meeting. She had changed into jeans and a sweater that was the same deep blue as her eyes. It looked terrific with her thick, curly blonde hair. Shannon is medium tall, with medium skin that tans easily. She always wears black mascara.

Logan Bruno, our other associate member, is from Kentucky originally. He's a sports fiend like me. He'll play just about any sport. But his favorites are basketball, track, and football, in spite of my efforts to convince him that soccer is what real football is all about.

Logan has blue eyes and curly blond-brown hair. He's average height and athletically built. Like me, he has an athlete's tan from being outside year-round. In addition to being the only guy in the BSC, he is one of only two BSC members who are dating other BSC members.

Mary Anne is the other, of course. They've been a couple for awhile now, which explains that V-day Dance question Claudia fired at Mary Anne the moment Mary Anne walked in the door.

"What are you going to wear?" Claudia asked now.

I groaned. Loudly.

No one seemed to notice. Mary Anne said, "I haven't decided yet."

Fortunately the phone rang and we had to spend a few minutes setting up a baby-sitting job. But the moment Kristy had called the Kormans back and confirmed the appointment,

Stacey picked up where Claudia had left off.

"I called Ethan this weekend," she confessed. "He's going to try to come to the dance." Ethan, Stacey's latest boyfriend, is an artist who lives in New York City. He's fifteen.

"Josh and I are definitely going to do the Valentine boogie-woogie," Claudia announced, looking pleased.

Jessi raised one eyebrow. Her focus is primarily on dancing, and while she's a little more enthusiastic about dating than Kristy or me, she's not the couples advocate that Claudia, Stacey, and Mary Anne are. She's basically decided she's not ready yet for the boyfriend-girlfriend thing.

"What about you, Kristy?" asked Claudia. I saw Mary Anne's quick, worried glance in Kristy's direction and guessed she was concerned that Claudia's question might be a little tactless. After all, the romance (if you could call it that) between Kristy and her former boyfriend and rival softball coach, Bart Taylor, had not ended well at all.

Sure enough, Kristy scowled. "What *about* me?" she said.

Claudia took the hint and looked for a quick way to change the subject. Her attention shifted to me and she said hastily, "Well, maybe Abby has someone with date potential lined up."

25

This caught me by surprise.

"Huh?" I said.

"Ross Brown," said Claudia.

"Ross who?" I answered.

Stacey snorted. Claudia rolled her eyes. "Abby! You were talking to him after school today, by your locker."

"Oh. Him," I said.

"He was laughing," put in Stacey. "He looked as if he was having fun talking to you."

"Of course he was," I said. "I was being funny. But what does that have to do with anything?"

"He might ask you to the Valentine's Day Dance . . . or you might ask him," Mary Anne suggested. A pretty bold suggestion, I thought, for someone so shy.

"I don't *think* so," I said with all the scorn I could muster. To Shannon I said, "You don't do this dumb dance stuff at your school, do you?"

Shannon wrinkled her nose, but her eyes were laughing. "Yeah, we do. But if I go, I'm just going to go with a bunch of friends."

Kristy said in a loud, impatient, let's-change-the-subject voice, "Speaking of dogs, Scout is almost ready to graduate."

Another worried look from Mary Anne met this announcement. "Oh, Kristy, really?" she said. For a moment I thought her eyes were going to fill with tears, but they didn't.

We all looked solemn, though.

Scout is the chocolate Labrador puppy that Kristy's family has been raising for the Guide Dog Foundation. That means that as a puppy-walker family (that's the official name for a family that raises a Guide Dog Foundation puppy) they agreed to take care of the puppy and train her, according to special and very specific rules, until she is old enough to go back to the foundation to learn to be a guide dog.

"It's going to be hard to say good-bye to Scout," said Jessi. "She's a great dog."

"I know," Kristy agreed. "But we've known all along that we'd have to give her back. Only I don't think David Michael or Karen, or Andrew or Emily quite realized what that meant. David Michael was saying the other day that maybe Scout wouldn't be chosen to be a guide dog. That happens every once in awhile, you know."

"But it's not likely, is it?" I asked.

Shaking her head, Kristy said, "No. This is going to be tough."

The phone rang again and this time everyone was relieved to hear it. We stopped talking about saying good-bye to Scout and about the Valentine's Day Dance, at least for a little while.

CHAPTER 3

By the next morning, dance mania at Stoney-brook Middle School was in full swing. PDAs (that's Public Displays of Affection) were rampant. Walking through the halls was like walking through the set of some bad romance movie: kissing, hand-holding, arm-locking, blushing, and flirting were everywhere.

Ugh.

Then, in English class, our new teacher for this semester, Ms. Colley — whom I'd liked up until now — announced with a big smile that we were going to study Shakespeare's sonnets. "These are some of the most beautiful and romantic poems in the English language," she announced.

I groaned. Loudly. And I am pleased to report that I was not the only one.

Ms. Colley beamed. "Emily," she said to Emily Bernstein, "please turn to page one-twenty-six in your textbook and read Sonnet Number Eighteen."

Emily gulped, stood up, and cleared her throat. She began to read in a solemn voice: " 'Shall I compare thee to a summer's day?/ Thou are more lovely and more temperate.' "

Naturally, since Emily is a good student, she read very well. Pete Black didn't read so well. He rushed through the rest of the sonnet and did not look happy. The snickers from some of his friends when he read certain words didn't help the situation.

But I noticed that many if not most of the girls in our class, including Emily, were giving Pete their complete attention.

Double ugh.

And it only grew worse when Ms. Colley encouraged us to discuss the sonnet.

Erica Blumberg, normally a funny, interesting person (she once won my personal Best Excuse for Not Doing Homework Award for telling the teacher that her mother had composted it), raised her hand and said, "It's about true love. Real, true love."

Jacqui Grant, a punkesque type whose claim to fame is green streaked hair, a nose ring, and the fact that she once got snagged by security guards while drinking at a concert, added to my dismay by saying, "It's like the lyrics of a great song, you know?" She then rattled off the words of one of U4Me's lame love rants.

Ms. Colley practically levitated. "Excellent connection, Jacqui! Just as rock music speaks to people of our era, Shakespeare was the voice of the people in his era."

"You mean people went around talking like that?" Pete looked horrified.

Margie Greene, an SMS cheerleader and a hugely popular student who at the moment was going steady with a ninth-grade track star, sighed. "It's not about how they talk. It's about how they really, truly feel." Her hand went up to touch the necklace she was wearing. It didn't take a rocket scientist to guess that Steady Boyfriend had given it to her.

I couldn't take it anymore. I raised my hand.

"Abby?" said Ms. Colley.

"If you're comparing love to a summer's day, you should also remember that summer days are nice, but they don't last forever," I said. "They end. They're just part of the whole year. Don't forget fall. And winter. And even spring. Don't forget hurricanes and tornadoes and floods. Don't forget earthquakes and —"

"I believe you've made your point," Ms. Colley interrupted me.

Ross Brown, who sits in the back of the room and is not usually what you'd call a big class participant, raised his hand. "Abby's right," he said. "True love encompasses more than just the sunny summer days. It is about being true through the hard times as well."

I wasn't sure that was exactly what I had said, but it was nice to have support. I nodded.

"A good point," conceded Ms. Colley. Then, as several girls opened their mouths to protest, she said, "Let's discuss the imagery in the poem a little more specifically, shall we?"

Although it didn't sink back to the syrup and saccharine level at which it had begun, that class will never rate among my favorites. I was very glad when it was over.

"Some class, huh?" Ross asked, stopping by my desk on the way out.

"The worst," I agreed. Where was my math homework? My perfect math homework, certified correct by Stacey McGill herself?

"I'm glad at least one other person in here feels the same way I do," Ross went on.

There was my math homework! Whew.

"Yeah," I said. "Valentine's Day is turning everyone's brains to mush. I mean, the dance is a week and a half away and that's all anybody can talk about. Don't people have lives?"

"You have more interesting things to do, I guess."

"Believe it," I told him.

"I don't care about the dance either," Ross

said as we walked out of the room. "I prefer something more low-key."

Ms. Frost, my math teacher, was going to be amazed when she saw my homework. I was actually looking forward to class. Math, I decided, was like soccer — you did better when you were prepared.

I realized we'd stopped outside the door to Ms. Colley's room. "Gotta go," I said.

"Want me to walk you?"

I laughed. "Don't worry. I know the way. See ya."

I hustled toward my next class, holding my math homework like a flag, no creative excuses required.

CHAPTER 4

The violin was violining when I got home, which meant that Anna was practicing. She is rigorous about practicing every day, as rigorous as Jessi is about ballet.

I tossed my books on my desk, still feeling all warm and fuzzy about the "excellent job" Ms. Frost had bestowed on me. It more than erased the bad feeling that Ms. Colley's class had given me.

"Shall I compare thy class to a winter's day?" I mentally addressed Ms. Colley. "Thou art more drippy and more disgusting."

I went back downstairs to the kitchen to seek nourishment.

The violin stopped.

Footsteps sounded on the stairs and along the hall to the kitchen. Anna said, "Abby? Is that you?"

"No, it's Mia Hamm."

Anna entered the kitchen, her brow furrowed. "Who?"

"The uh, the . . . Stradivari of soccer players, that's who."

"Oh. A good soccer player. I get it," she said.

Stradivari, in case you didn't know, made famous fiddles long, long ago. Oh, excuse me, *violins*. They are worth gazillions of dollars today.

"The *best* soccer player," I corrected her.

I was a little surprised that Anna had stopped her music-making to join me. She usually doesn't. In fact, we usually don't do any bonding until dinner, when Mom comes home.

"Heard any good music lately?" I said.

It was feeble, but Anna smiled. I pulled a bag of microwave popcorn off the shelf and started nuking it. While it was popping, I poured out some Gatorade. When I offered some to Anna, she shook her head and wrinkled her nose.

"You're right," I said. "It's an acquired taste. Want a soda?"

"Put some water on for hot tea," she suggested.

"Okay."

When the popcorn, Gatorade, and hot tea were on the table, I sat down across from Anna. She wrapped her hands around her mug and stared at the tea bag.

"You're taking up fortune-telling?" I asked.

She shook her head. You didn't have to be Anna's twin to sense that she was a little down.

"Well, I can predict the future. I predict that for the next week or so — until the Valentine's Day Dance — everyone at SMS will totally lose their minds except you and me."

"I'm not so sure about me," Anna murmured.

"What?"

She shrugged.

I said, "You haven't bought into the madness, have you? Sucking face in the hall? Desperately seeking dance date? Spending entire English classes talking about *romance*?" My voice was going up. I couldn't help myself.

With a laugh, Anna said, "No! Come on, Abby. You know me better than that."

"I hope I do." I eyed her suspiciously.

Anna took a sip of tea. "It's just that, well, going to the dance might be kind of fun."

"More fun than listening to everybody talk about it, maybe," I muttered.

"Dances are fun, Abby. Having someone special to do things with could be fun too."

Trying to be reasonable and sympathetic, I said, "You could go to the dance."

"I don't have a date."

"You don't have to have a date. Just go with friends. Lots of people do that. Jessi is going to. Shannon is, at her school."

Anna shrugged.

"What about some of the people in the school orchestra? You could go with them."

Again, Anna shrugged. I realized that she wasn't comfortable with the idea. Neither of us has a *lot* of friends, but I at least have the BSC to backstop me. If I wanted to go to the dance, I'd feel fine about asking any or all of them to make it into a team effort. Anna clearly didn't feel the same way about her musical friends.

Abruptly, she stood up. "Oh, well," she said. "It's no big deal."

"You're right. It isn't." I made a face.

Anna made a face back. Then she went upstairs to continue her violin practice, leaving me to nurse my Gatorade and consider the possibility that for some people, the Valentine's Day Dance was a serious event — and not having a date was a real problem.

Weird.

Maybe it was the conversation with Anna, but when I reached SMS the next day and cruised the romance-saturated halls to my locker, I didn't feel quite so cranky about it all. Oh, I still didn't think Public Displays of Affection were necessary. In fact, I think for the most part they are downright low-rent.

But hey, let Cupid worry about that.

I did notice that some people seemed a little

over-the-top about their couple status, and I don't just mean PDAs. I mean, the way some guys and girls clung to each other, they looked as if they were afraid they'd die or something if they let go.

These were the people who seriously needed to get lives.

But other people made a nice argument for being part of a couple. I spotted Mary Anne and Logan by Logan's locker. He was leaning against it, talking to Mary Anne, and she was smiling and gesturing as she answered. You could tell by the way they interacted that they were good friends and a good couple, even though they weren't engaged in any kind of lip lock or body twining.

I passed Claudia's locker a on my way to my first class and she motioned to me, grinning. "Check this out," she said. Then she added simply, "Josh."

Josh had given Claudia's locker a new look. It reminded me of the Valentine's Day locker decor at my old school. He'd bought a box of those valentines that little kids give one another and had strung them together on red ribbon to loop back and forth across the front of Claud's locker. In between, he'd hung individually wrapped valentine candies: Hershey's Kisses, Reese's peanut butter cups, and I don't know what else.

Claudia, her cheek bulging from one of her early morning candy-grams, said a little thickly, "This is *so* cool. Want one?"

"No thanks," I said. "But it was a sweet thought."

"Yes," Claudia agreed with a little sigh, either ignoring or missing the joke completely. "It was."

I left her to finish collecting her candy and went to class. Josh, I decided, might be perfect for Claudia. Maybe it really was true love . . . or at least, a long summer's day.

At lunch, Stacey announced that Ethan had sent her "the most romantic e-mail."

"Stop right there," I said. "E-mail and romance do not belong in the same sentence."

"You'd change your mind if you could see what he wrote," Stacey said.

"Try me," I suggested.

Stacey actually blushed a little. "N-No," she said. "All you need to know is that he's coming to the dance."

"Excellent!" Claudia cried.

"That's nice," I said, trying to be neutral.

In English class, Ms. Colley continued to lead us in a romantic exploration of the sonnets of Shakespeare.

At one point, Emily raised her hand. "Ms. Colley," she said. "What about the *Sonnets from the Portuguese*? You know, the ones by Elizabeth Barrett Browning."

Ms. Colley lit up like the Christmas tree at Rockefeller Center. "Ah!" she said. "Those sonnets include one I am sure all of you have heard."

Emily nodded. "I have it here," she said, laying her hand reverently on a small book on her desk.

"Please," said Ms. Colley. "Share it with the class."

Emily stood up, opened the book, turned the pages carefully, and began to read:

" 'How do I love thee? Let me count the ways.
I love thee to the depth and breadth and height
My soul can reach, when feeling out of sight
For the ends of Being and ideal Grace . . .' "

I saw nods of recognition. Jacqui made a face but leaned forward and looked at Emily intently as Emily read.

I groaned. Loudly. Ms. Colley's eyes flicked in my direction.

When Emily had finished, Ms. Colley said, "Elizabeth Barrett Browning is writing about her love for her husband, Robert Browning, himself a poet. Theirs is a great and true love story."

She told the story, which, as far as I could tell, went like this: Lizzie Barrett hung around on a sofa being a poet and enjoying ill health until the Robster came along. Then she fell in love with him and jumped up off the sofa — because love cures all.

Only, if you ask me, she probably just replaced one sickness with another: lovesickness.

I yawned.

Ms. Colley's eyes flicked toward me again. "Yes, Abby? You have something you'd like to share with the class?"

Did I ever! "Obsessive," I said. "That's what it sounds like to me. She's obsessed with this guy. I mean, it sounds creepy. She's almost like one of those wackos who follow people around and watch them — "

"Okay, Abby," Ms. Colley stepped in.

"What Abby's saying, and I agree," Ross spoke up, "is that this sounds like an unhealthy love."

"This is poetry, Ross," said Ms. Colley. "I believe you could safely say that she is using extravagant language and extravagant imagery, for the sake of effect. But why don't we talk about some of the images Barrett Browning and Shakespeare used? How do you think their use of imagery compares?"

Folding my arms, I sank back in my seat. Clearly, Ms. Colley was as besotted with love and Valentine's Day madness as all the rest of SMS.

When Ross stopped by my desk after class, I said, "Ms. Colley doesn't want to hear it, does she? I mean, puh-lease! Give me a break!"

"It *is* a little over-the-top. But if you don't take it too seriously, Valentine's Day can be fun," he said.

"Maybe. I'm trying to maintain an ironic distance," I replied. I wasn't quite sure what I meant, but it sounded good.

Ross nodded. "Of course, sonnets like this don't mean that romance doesn't exist in the real world."

"I know. That's not the problem. The problem is the way everybody thinks it's the only thing on earth, you know?"

"So you *do* agree that romance is not a bad thing," Ross said.

We'd made it to the hall. Time to go to math class. Since I didn't have a perfect homework paper to flaunt in front of Ms. Frost, I didn't mind lingering a little. "Romance is not a bad thing, in its place."

"Like the Valentine's Day Dance," Ross said.

"Yeah, I guess," I conceded.

"So you want to go?"

"Go where?" For a moment, I thought Ross was talking about class. Then I saw him duck his head.

"To the dance," he said to his feet. "With me."

"The Valentine's Day Dance? Here at SMS?" I was incredulous.

"Yes," he said.

"No," I said.

He looked surprised. He looked taken aback. He looked hurt.

Maybe I'd been a little rude. "Ross," I began, "I truly don't buy into all this stuff. Nothing personal, but I'm just not that kind of person."

"Yeah, I know," he said, recovering. "Just checking."

"Did I pass the antiromance test?" I joked.

"Yup."

"Good. I have to go. See you," I said.

Feeling a little weird about our exchange, I turned and walked toward math class. I happened to look back just before I turned the corner.

Ross still stood there, staring after me.

In my mind, I began composing a new sonnet. It was called, "To Valentine's Day" and it began, "How do I detest thee? Let me count the ways."

CHAPTER 5

Friday

Scout isn't gone yet, but I think she might be more ready to leave her first home than at least one of your siblings thinks she is, Kristy. It's a good thing I came prepared with a secret weapon. It helped to distract Andrew and Karen and David Michael, at least for the time being....

On Friday afternoon, Kristy was on her way to a Sports Committee meeting for the softball team, even though it was the middle of the winter. So Mary Anne went to Kristy's house to sit for Karen, Andrew, and David Michael until the BSC meeting, when Nannie (who was running errands with Emily Michelle) would be back to take over.

Mary Anne was expecting to have fun, especially since she hadn't seen Andrew for awhile. He had only recently returned to the big house, as he and his sister call Watson's mansion, after spending several months in Chicago with his mom and stepfather. And Karen's ever-active imagination could always be counted on as a source of entertainment.

Mary Anne was also rather pleased with her foresight. She had called Mrs. Brewer and arranged for her to buy certain items for a special baby-sitting project Mary Anne had planned.

Nannie had just finished buttoning and zipping Emily Michelle into layers and layers of winter clothing when Mary Anne arrived.

"Here, I'll finish that," Mary Anne volunteered.

"Thanks," Nannie said, and began to pull on a coat, a hat, gloves, and a scarf. She was pretty well bundled up but not as thickly wrapped as Emily, whose arms were sticking almost straight out thanks to the layers of clothes she was wearing.

"Emily Michelle doesn't like the cold," Nannie said, hoisting Emily to her hip. "Say 'bye-'bye, sweetie."

Emily's mitten moved slightly. " 'Bye," she said.

" 'Bye, Emily Michelle," replied Mary Anne.

"Grocery store, then the hardware store, and that may take awhile," Nannie said crisply. "Phone numbers are posted by the telephone, but we should be back no later than five."

"I think Kristy is going straight from school to the BSC meeting," Mary Anne reminded Nannie.

Nannie nodded. "And Charlie is supposed to give you a ride. Kristy already told me. Several times. She told Charlie too." Nannie and Mary Anne exchanged a smile that said, *Of course she did*.

By this time, the rest of the family had realized that Mary Anne had arrived. Karen, David Michael, and Andrew came charging toward her as she walked down the hall. Following them was Shannon, the Bernese mountain dog puppy, and Scout.

"Hi, hi, hi!" Karen shouted, hurling herself at Mary Anne. Not to be outdone, David Michael high-fived her. Shannon leaped up and barked.

Andrew hung back a little. He smiled at Mary Anne, but he kept one hand on Scout. Scout stood calmly, her tail wagging, and waited for Mary Anne to say hello to her.

"Come see Pumpkin! She's all black! That's why she's Pumpkin, the Halloween cat!" Karen said. She wasn't talking as loudly as she could (that would be her outdoor voice), but she managed to fill her indoor voice with plenty of exclamation marks.

Mary Anne bent to pet Scout and say hello to Andrew. "How are you guys doing?" she asked.

"My dog is fine," Andrew answered in a clear voice. "Come on, Scout. Karen wants to show Mary Anne her kitten."

My dog? Her kitten?

Karen slipped a hand into Mary Anne's. "Pumpkin likes me best," she confided in a very soft voice, especially for her. "But she's not my kitten. She belongs to all of us."

"If Pumpkin likes you best," David Michael said practically, "then that makes you Pumpkin's person. It's just the same as Pumpkin being your kitten."

We reached the family room and Karen cooed, "Pumpkin, purr, kitty."

Immediately, a half-grown midnight-black kitten levitated up to the back of the sofa, arched her spine, tiptoed cat-style to the end of the sofa back, and then said, "Mrrrow?"

She looked at Karen as she did so. She had amazing eyes.

"Mrrroooow." This time, it was clearly a statement and not a question.

"She's saying, 'Pick me up and pet me. Now,' " Karen interpreted, then did just that.

The moment Karen lifted Pumpkin to her shoulder, Pumpkin began to purr.

David Michael stroked the soft fur, and so did Mary Anne.

"Isn't she soft?" David Michael said.

"Mrr, mrrow," said Pumpkin.

"She talks a lot," Karen said. "Maybe she has some Siamese in her. Siamese cats talk lots."

"Woof!" That was Shannon. David Michael immediately dropped to his knees. "You're soft too, Shanny," he crooned. "Good girl. You're the best."

By this time, Mary Anne had realized that Andrew was not participating in the pet love fest. In fact, he wasn't even in the room.

"Andrew? Andrew!"

Andrew came into the family room and held out his hand. "I brought treats for Pumpkin," he explained. "She likes these a lot."

"Thanks, Andrew," said Karen. Andrew held up a treat, and Pumpkin put out her paw to touch his hand as she gobbled up the treat.

Then Andrew turned. "Scout likes treats too, don't you, Scout?"

"Andrew, wait!" said David Michael.

But Andrew had already tossed a cat treat into the air. "Catch!" he said.

The treat bounced off Scout's head. Shannon scooped it up while Scout was still looking around to see what had hit her.

"Andrew, NO!" Karen shouted in her outdoor voice.

Mary Anne didn't bother to remind Karen to use her indoor voice. Karen was right. Scout wasn't supposed to be trained to expect treats tossed to her or be rewarded for good behavior with food.

If she was, she might never become a guide dog, because a dog that is governed by its nose and stomach wouldn't make a very reliable guide dog, for obvious reasons.

Andrew said, "It's not fair. Shannon gets treats. Pumpkin gets treats."

"We don't give Shannon treats in front of Scout," David Michael pointed out.

Sticking out his lower lip, Andrew said, "Well, it's not fair."

With the keen instincts of a seasoned babysitter, Mary Anne realized that there was more at stake here than feeding Scout treats. Of all of

Kristy's siblings, Andrew was the one who was obviously having the most trouble accepting Scout's imminent departure.

"Speaking of treats," said Mary Anne, "I brought something special for us."

"Is it candy?" Karen asked, diverted. She added, "Candy is bad for dogs. Especially chocolate."

"It's not candy and it's not people treats either," Mary Anne replied, leading the way to the kitchen. "It's a surprise." She opened the refrigerator and was relieved to see a key ingredient in her surprise resting on one shelf of the refrigerator: beef suet.

"Good," said Mary Anne.

"What's good?" asked David Michael.

"What's the surprise?" Andrew asked.

"First we have to go on an expedition," said Mary Anne. "Everybody put on your coats and gloves and hats."

"It's cold outside," Andrew objected. "I don't want to go out, and neither does Scout. Do you, Scout?"

Hearing her name, Scout wagged her tail and looked expectantly at Andrew. Mary Anne could tell what an intelligent, calm dog she was becoming.

"Want to go for a walk, Shannon?" David Michael asked.

Shannon's response was a happy dance that involved running to the back door, where the leashes hung on a hook, and back to David Michael.

Scout's tail picked up its tempo, but she didn't run and leap like Shannon.

"Andrew, you and Scout will have to come with us," Mary Anne said firmly. "We can't leave you here. We won't be outside long."

"Oh, all right," said Andrew.

Mary Anne helped Karen into her coat and turned to find that Andrew had bundled himself up, but that Scout wasn't wearing her special dog vest with the words GUIDE DOG IN TRAINING on it. Knowing that Scout was supposed to wear it every time she went out for a walk, Mary Anne looked around. "Where's Scout's vest?"

"She doesn't need it." Andrew scowled.

"She's supposed to wear it every time she goes out, Andrew," said Karen sternly. Karen is a stickler for rules, which can be a pain sometimes, but isn't a bad quality when it comes to dog training.

"She doesn't want to be a guide dog," said Andrew. "She just wants to stay with me and be happy."

Mary Anne thought fast and said, "But it's cold out, Andrew, and Scout's coat isn't as thick as Shannon's. Don't you think she should wear her vest?"

For a long moment, Andrew hesitated. Then he said, "Oh, okay. Just this once."

After convincing Karen that Pumpkin didn't want to go for a walk, and telling her that she could be in charge of the "collection bag," Mary Anne at last led the kids outside. David Michael led Shannon on her leash; Andrew was holding onto Scout's leash with one hand and Mary Anne's hand with the other; and Karen clutched a net grocery bag.

"What are we collecting?" Karen asked.

"Pinecones," said Mary Anne. She looked around. "Has anybody seen any?"

"In Morbidda Destiny's front yard!" Karen said, her eyes wide. Karen has dubbed Mrs. Porter, who lives next door, Morbidda Destiny. And she's more than half convinced herself and her siblings that Mrs. Porter is a witch.

"And in Abby and Anna's yard too. Next to their driveway," added David Michael.

"That sounds good. Let's walk the dogs around the block, and then we can gather pinecones," suggested Mary Anne.

As they walked the dogs, Mary Anne fended off questions about what the pinecones were for. "I'll tell you when we get back to the house with them," she promised. "For now, all you need to know is that the cones can't be too brittle or opened up too wide. They should be sort of half folded shut."

When they had circled the block, they stopped by the pine tree near the sidewalk in front of Mrs. Porter's house.

"Scout and I will keep witch watch," Andrew said. He turned to stare at Mrs. Porter's big, old house. Mary Anne had to admit that in its dark, run-down state, it did look like a drawing of a haunted house from a children's picture book. But she also knew that Mrs. Porter wasn't a witch.

When they'd picked up all the perfect pinecones they could find by the sidewalk, they walked to my yard. Andrew helped pick up pinecones there, holding each one down for Scout to examine before putting it into the bag Karen was holding.

Mary Anne noticed that although Shannon still didn't have her leash manners down exactly — she had a tendency to pull toward anything that interested her, though not as hard as she once had — Scout didn't pull at all. And she was a big enough dog now to pull Andrew anywhere she wanted to go. But she stayed by his side.

They returned to the house with a bulging bag of pinecones, probably many more than they would need. But Mary Anne figured that the exercise was good for everyone and that they could do more sorting when they reached the kitchen.

Inside, they spread newspapers on the kitchen table and swathed themselves in aprons. Then Mary Anne put the kids to work tying loops of yarn to the tops of the pinecones. Meanwhile, Mary Anne put the beef suet in a pan and began melting it over low heat into a sort of jelly. When it was mostly melted, she stirred in a big glob of peanut butter.

"Eeewwww," said Karen. "I'm not eating *that*. That looks like a recipe from a witch's cookbook."

"Actually, it's a recipe from a bird book," said Mary Anne. "David Michael, would you please get the birdseed? It's by the back door."

David Michael and Karen poured some birdseed into a shallow bowl that Mary Anne had set on the table. When the suet–peanut butter mix was cool enough not to burn anybody, but still jellylike, Mary Anne set the saucepan on a trivet on the table. She picked a pinecone out of the bag, held it up, and made a big show of examining it, then twirled it in the jellylike goo.

Handing the sticky pinecone to Karen, Mary Anne said, "Now, roll it in the birdseed."

"Bird snacks!" cried David Michael.

"That's right."

"See, Andrew?" said David Michael, taking

the next pinecone from Mary Anne. "After you roll it in birdseed, you can hang it in a tree, and the birds can eat the seeds and the, uh . . ."

"Peanut butter surprise," Karen supplied.

Andrew looked more interested and less unhappy than he had all day. Soon all four of them were making birdseed pinecones as fast as they could, lining up the finished ones on the newspaper.

When they'd used up all the goo, they took the treats outside. (Karen insisted on saving all the unused cones for future bird-food projects.) Then they decorated the tree outside the family room window with bird feeder pinecones. There were a few left over. Mary Anne put them in a covered bowl, labeled it BIRD FOOD in big letters, and set it in the refrigerator.

Then they went back inside to wait for the birds to arrive. "Come to dinner," called Karen. "Come on, birds."

A black-capped chickadee appeared as if by magic, attached itself to a pinecone, and began to peck as the cone bobbed on the branch.

"Bird television," David Michael said, grinning at Mary Anne.

"And every new bird is like changing the channel," agreed Karen.

They watched "bird television" until Nannie came home, and Charlie arrived to take Mary Anne and me to the BSC meeting. Mary Anne noticed that all afternoon Andrew stayed near Scout, one hand resting on her collar.

When Mary Anne told us about this later, she didn't need to add that Andrew was going to have trouble letting go of Scout. Everything he'd done all afternoon had made it clear that "Good-bye, Scout" was not part of his vocabulary.

CHAPTER 6

"It's true. Andrew's been sticking to Scout like glue ever since he came back from Chicago," said Kristy.

"It's not easy going back and forth between your parents, even when they are as nice as Watson and Lisa," Stacey said. (Lisa is Andrew and Karen's mom.)

"I know," Mary Anne said. "Look at how hard it was on Dawn."

We were quiet for a moment, thinking over what Mary Anne had told us about her baby-sitting job with Karen, Andrew, and David Michael.

"Maybe . . . " Jessi's voice trailed off.

We all looked at her. She continued, "Well, maybe Andrew feels sort of like Scout. You know, Scout leaves. Andrew leaves. Maybe he's worried that if Scout can go away and not come back, that could happen to him too."

"It's a possibility," said Kristy thoughtfully.

"He also wants something of his own," I pointed out. "That's pretty obvious. A big pet to call his own." Andrew has a goldfish and a hermit crab — neither of which you can pet, take for a walk, or hang out with like you can with, say, a dog.

"True," Kristy agreed. "But that's not going to happen. At least, I don't think Mom and Watson are ready for any more animals."

The phone rang then, and we went into appointment-making mode. After we'd scheduled the sitting job, I said, "Speaking of Valentine's Day . . ."

"Were we? Speaking of Valentine's Day?" asked Claudia.

"As far as I can tell, that's all anybody's been speaking of lately," I retorted. "Anyway, listen to this. You were right about Ross Brown. He actually asked me to the Valentine's Day Dance! At first I thought he was joking. In fact, maybe he was. I mean, we both laughed after I said no."

"*No,*" Claudia echoed blankly. "You said no?"

"Yes. I mean, of course I said no. I don't dance. Not at the Valentine's Day Dance, anyway."

"You're kidding. I mean, don't you like Ross? He's nice. He's cute. He's funny," said Stacey.

"Then *you* go with him," I shot back, feeling a little defensive, in case you couldn't tell.

Stacey continued, "Even if you don't like him that much, you could go to the dance with him. Have some fun. Maybe meet a really cute guy there who you do like."

"So you think Abby should use Ross to meet other guys?" Kristy was *not* amused.

"No! But I mean, it's just a dance. It's not as if Ross asked Abby to marry him or anything," Stacey said.

I snorted. "A good thing too."

Jessi said, "Maybe someone else will ask you, who you like better. You're right, though, it's no big deal."

"No matter who asked me, I'd still say no. Even Cam Geary." I directed this last sentence at Mary Anne, because I could see she was about to weigh in with her opinion. Cam Geary is a TV star and, according to Mary Anne, the cutest guy on the planet — except for Logan, of course, who allegedly looks like Cam anyway.

"Even Cam Geary would have his feelings hurt, I think, if you turned him down the way you say you turned Ross down," Mary Anne said.

"Look, I'm not going to lie or make fake excuses, okay? I don't want to go to the dance, *and* I don't want to go to the dance with Ross.

There are a few other things in life besides the Valentine's Day Dance, you know."

Mary Anne, ever the peacemaker, said, "Well, anyway, it's nice to be asked, isn't it?"

I wanted to roll my eyes, but I didn't. "Yeah," I said. "Sure."

Brrinng! Saved by the phone once again, I settled back, with a sigh, in my chair in the corner. Were we finished with the Ross–Valentine's Day Dance subject? Somehow, I didn't think so.

I'd barely walked in the door after the BSC meeting when Anna called from the kitchen, "Abby?"

"I'll be there to help in just a minute. I'm not late!" I was feeling belligerent.

Anna said, "I know you're not. I just came down myself. All we have to do tonight is set the table."

At breakfast, Mom had promised to bring home a "city picnic," which meant she would go to one of her favorite kosher places, Russ & Daughters, to buy all kinds of goodies.

"Oh. Right," I said. "Sorry. I've had a bad afternoon, sort of. Maybe even a bad day." I went into the kitchen.

"Well, I have some news that will cheer you up." Anna's eyes were sparkling.

"Mom bought tickets to the next women's World Cup?"

"No." Anna shook her head. "Better than that."

"I'm stumped. I can't imagine what would be better than that . . . except playing on a World Cup team."

Anna laughed. "Ross Brown is going to ask you to the Valentine's Day Dance!"

She waited breathlessly for my reaction.

I hated to disappoint her, but what could I do?

"Old news," I said flippantly. "He did, and I'm not."

"Not?"

"Not going. To the dance. With Ross. Or anyone." I opened a drawer, took out silverware, and began to set the table.

"You're *kidding*!" Anna cried.

I winced. "Indoor voice," I muttered.

Anna ignored me. "You said *no*?"

I told her the story. It was, I thought, a funny story. But for the second time that day, I didn't get a laugh. (This proves, conclusively and forever, that "identical twins" aren't necessarily identical inside out.)

"I don't believe it," said my humorless sister.

"What?" I said. "How did you find out, anyway? Are you on his side? Did he sign you up for the Give Abby Grief and Make Her Go to the Dance Committee?"

"No. I mean, I've barely ever even spoken to Ross. But he's friends with a girl in my cello section, and she told me. And he's nice. He's funny. He'd be a great date."

"Not for me," I said. "Ross is fine, but I don't like him in that way. Never have, never will. *And* let me make it extra clear: I'm not interested in dating Ross or *anyone*. End of story."

I slammed the final fork down on the table.

"Oh, Abby," said Anna. "You could have gone to the dance."

"Tell Ross's friend to tell Ross to ask me to the women's World Cup, then I'll go. Maybe." I walked out of the kitchen, exasperated. Everyone had indeed gone crazy.

I wished Ross had never asked me to the dance. I wished I'd never told anybody he had. What a rotten way to start the weekend.

Upstairs, in my room, I pressed my forehead to the cold windowpane and beamed a message out across the sky: *Ross*, I thought. *Ask someone else to the dance.*

Soon.

CHAPTER 7

I woke up the next morning and for no reason at all thought, *Maybe I'll go over to Kristy's house.*

This is not my usual Saturday morning behavior. Kristy and I ride the school bus together, I'm her assistant coach for the Krushers softball team (made up of kids whose average age is 5.8, many of whom play with more enthusiasm than skill), we both like sports, *but* we are not that close. Kristy's bossy.

And I'm not into being the boss-ee.

That's a joke, in case you didn't notice.

But with my own twin giving me "Have you lost your mind?" looks, I felt in need of someone who wasn't Valentine's Day Dance–addled. As far as I could tell, that someone was Kristy.

Naturally, her whole house was already in gear when I arrived, even though it was early. In fact, I met Kristy and Watson out front. Watson was holding Scout's leash while she, um, went on command. That was one of the first things that the guide dog school encouraged Kristy and her family to teach Scout — to relieve herself in a specific spot and on command. That way, when she was partnering a blind person, or someone whose sight was impaired, she would be able to go on command, rather than trotting off to the nearest patch of interesting-smelling grass with her person in tow.

"Good girl, Scout," Watson was saying as I approached.

At that moment the front door banged open, and Andrew came hurtling out, with Kristy's mom behind him. "Andrew, wait! You don't have a coat on."

"Scout's mine!" he shouted, grabbing for the leash. "I'm supposed to walk her."

"You can walk her back inside," Watson said calmly, handing Andrew the leash.

"Come on, Scout," said Andrew. He glared at Watson and Kristy, included me for good measure, then led the chocolate Lab back inside past Mrs. Brewer, who was shaking her head.

As I reached the door, I saw the two adults exchange a glance.

"I could use another cup of coffee," said Watson.

"Decaf," Kristy reminded him. Watson had a very mild heart attack not long ago. And even though he takes care of himself and follows doctor's orders, and although Kristy's mom is there for backup, Kristy can't suppress her natural take-charge instincts.

"Decaf," Watson agreed with a smile.

"You hungry?" Kristy transferred her attention to me.

"Already bageled. With cream cheese. And lox," I said.

"Well, I need to English muffin," Kristy said, then grinned. "Come on, you can keep me company."

Kristy's mother and stepfather headed for the kitchen table.

"Anyone else want an English muffin?" Kristy asked.

"No," said Watson. "Thanks."

Mrs. Brewer shook her head.

Andrew marched into the kitchen with Scout and Karen, who had Pumpkin on her shoulder.

"I'm hungry," said Andrew. "And so is my dog."

"Scout eats at night now," Karen reminded him. "Once a day."

"I can feed my dog when I want to," Andrew protested.

Mrs. Brewer put a hand out and caught Andrew gently by the arm as he headed for the pantry. She pulled him up onto her lap. "Andrew," she said, "Scout is fed at night. You know that. You help feed her."

"If you're hungry, I'll toast a muffin for you," Kristy said to me.

"Ah-choo," I said. "Allergies." My nose was becoming stuffy.

"Oh. Sorry!" said Karen. "Come on, Pumpkin. Come on, Scout."

They left, and Andrew started to slide out of Mrs. Brewer's lap. But she stopped him.

"You know, Andrew, that Scout belongs to the Guide Dog Foundation. We're only her family for a little while. In fact, we've done such a good job at helping her grow up that she's going to leave soon. She's ready to go to school, to learn to do her job."

I half expected Andrew to pitch a fit or something, but it was clear he had heard this before.

He said, "Send Shannon instead!"

"Shannon's a part of our family. David Michael and all of us would miss her if she went away." Kristy's mom stroked Andrew's forehead. "We raised Shannon to be our very own dog. We didn't raise Scout that way."

He pulled away from his stepmom's hand and slid out of her lap. He looked at his dad. "Karen has a kitten and David Michael has Shannon. I want a dog of my own."

"Bingo," I heard Kristy say under her breath. Our eyes met. I'd been right.

Watson put down his coffee cup. "This isn't a good time for a new dog, Andrew," he said. "We have a houseful of people and pets right now."

"Then don't give my dog away!" Andrew suddenly shouted at the top of his lungs. He ran out of the kitchen. "Scout! Scout! Here, girl!" we heard him calling.

Kristy's mom looked at Watson. "What are we going to do?" she said.

"I don't know," replied Watson, looking unhappy. He glanced at Kristy and me. "Any suggestions?"

But we didn't have a single one.

Holding Emily Michelle on one hip, I followed Kristy into the family room. Andrew was lying on his stomach on the floor, talking softly to Scout as he put a puzzle together. Karen and David Michael were staging some kind of drama involving Karen's dollhouse, their combined sets of toy farm animals, Pumpkin, and Shannon.

I sneezed.

Kristy said, "If we sit on the stairs, we can keep an eye on things, and you won't be in the same room with all the animals."

"Good idea," I agreed.

We each claimed a step and settled down.

"Poor Andrew," Kristy said softly. "He's such a, well, kid."

"A little boy," I agreed.

"Don't let him hear you say that," she warned me with a smile.

"*I* know." I smiled back. Then I sighed.

"Boys," I said.

"Tell me about it." Kristy groaned.

"Valentine's Day," I added.

"When everyone's brain turns the same consistency as those soft-centered chocolates," Kristy said.

"You know, I didn't *ask* Ross to like me," I said. "So why does everyone act as if I did something wrong when I told him no?"

Maybe I was overstating the case a little, but not much.

"Couples want other people to be in couples too," Kristy said. "Mary Anne, for instance, is happy with Logan, and she wants other people to have that. Especially her friends."

Aha! A rare moment of insight from Kristy Thomas, I thought. Aloud I said, "You don't have to be part of a couple to be happy."

"I know that, and you know that, but some people have a lot of growing up to do before they figure it out," Kristy said.

We were silent for a moment. Then, to my surprise, Kristy said, "Letting Ross know that you don't want to go out with him was the right thing to do, Abby."

"You think so?" I leaned back and stared at the ceiling.

"I know it. When I started sort of seeing Bart, it was because he was a good friend and I felt comfortable with him. But I think I knew all along that I was never going to, you know, feel romantic about him or anything."

"But you went to a dance with him. You did date stuff with him."

With a shrug, Kristy said, "Because it was easy to do. I mean, we did things with Mary Anne and Logan. Stacey and Claudia and even Jessi and Mal seemed to think it was great, so I . . . took the easy way out. And when I realized that I didn't want to be more than friends with Bart, he wasn't happy. I didn't just lose a date —I might have lost a friend too. I mean, he and I are still awfully careful around each other, not like real friends. And that's what really bothers me."

I stared at Kristy. She stared back, then made a goofy face.

I smiled. "Thanks," I said. I meant, thanks for talking about this, thanks for telling me, thanks for making me feel better. And, of course, thanks for being a friend.

CHAPTER 8

When I woke up on Sunday morning, I bounded out of bed the way I usually do, dragged on my sweats, and was about to put on my running shoes, when my brain finally registered the hiss of sleety snow against the windows. Realizing that the run I had planned would be an exercise in slip and fall, I flopped back onto my bed, sweats and all, and went back to sleep.

I slept late. I woke up, ate breakfast, and read the sports section and the comics while Mom yawned over hot tea and the *Times*. Then I went back to my room to do homework. I passed Anna on the stairs. She had managed to put on her jeans and an old sweater, but I could tell she was still half asleep. She mumbled something that sounded like "Ddmrnin," which I correctly translated as "Good morning."

"Good morning," I replied softly. I have

sympathy for people who wake up late and slowly, like my twin, even though I'm normally an early riser myself.

Feeling virtuous, I planted myself at my desk and reached for my homework. I opened the book to a nasty row of math problems that I'd been putting off. I heard, faintly, some strains of music and recognized one of Anna's favorite disks, Bach's Brandenburg Concertos. Not my cup of tea in the morning, but I guess it eased the transition to wakefulness for Anna. Mom seemed to like it too.

"Abby?" I heard Anna say a few minutes later.

I'd just focused in on a problem, but Anna's voice made me lose the connection. I ran both hands through my hair in frustration. Maybe if I ignored her . . .

"Abby!"

"Coming," I said.

I opened the door and called, "What? What is it?"

"You have company," Anna said in a funny voice.

So why didn't she just send up Kristy or whoever it was? I sighed in exasperation and thumped down the stairs.

Anna was standing in the front hall, smiling. At *Ross*. She laughed as I appeared, and Ross laughed with her. In spite of the fact that Anna is no morning glory, she looked positively animated all of a sudden.

"Ross," I said.

He turned, and I saw what he was holding: pink roses.

"Aren't they beautiful, Abby?" Anna cooed, stroking one of the velvet buds with a finger.

"Uh, yeah. They're ah, ahh, *ah-choo*!" I said and took a step back.

"Abby's a little allergic to things sometimes," Anna explained.

Ross didn't seem to hear her. He was looking at me with a funny expression on his face.

I realized then that in my old sweats and ratty slippers, with my hair sticking out like a bunch of live wires, I must have been a shocking sight. (Ha-ha!)

Good, I thought. That should cure Ross. This is the real me.

Ross said, "Abby, you look great. It's good to see you."

My heart sank. Anna pried the roses from Ross's hands and said, "I'll just go put these in water, okay?"

The sneeze-flowers left the hall, and I could breathe again. The only problem was, Ross was crowding my space. I mean, he was standing in *my* hall on a Sunday morning. Who had invited him anyway?

"My mom's a florist," Ross said. "She had

some extra roses, and I thought I'd drop them off."

"So you're on your way somewhere," I said.

"Yeah. Sort of."

Silence fell. I didn't want to encourage him.

But Ross didn't seem to notice my new mute policy. He cocked his head, listened, and said, "Bach. The Brandenburgs . . . I went to a concert the other night. The Albemarle Quintet. They did Bach's Concerto for . . ."

"It's Anna's," I interrupted. "Anna's music. I'm more or less tone-deaf."

"Oh," said Ross.

"So you see, I'm not into music *or* dances."

Ross laughed then, as if I'd said something really funny. "I bet you're a good dancer, Abby," he replied.

A car horn sounded.

I said, "I guess it's time for you to go."

"Right," said Ross. But he hesitated.

"Thanks for the roses," I said. "They're very . . . pink."

"Don't mention it. Anytime. See you at school."

"See you," I echoed, more or less herding him out the door. He turned to wave at the bottom of the steps, which made me feel rotten because I was aware that I'd been just a tad rude. I smiled at him and waved back with more warmth then I had intended — the smile and wave of a guilty person.

But guilty of what? Nothing except not wanting to date someone who wanted to date me.

Feeling more than a little annoyed, I stomped toward the kitchen just as Anna emerged, with the roses in a tall glass vase. "Is Ross gone already?" she asked, looking down the hall as if she expected to see him behind me.

I took a step back and held up my hands. Anna looked at the roses. "Oh," she said.

"Why don't you put them in your room?" I was going to tell her to throw them away, but since she'd already put them in a vase, I decided it would be a waste.

"Really?"

"They're all yours. I have to do my homework."

But I wasn't going to get away that easily. Anna followed me upstairs, holding the roses. "I'll put them on my dresser," she said. "They'll be reflected in the mirror. It'll be beautiful."

"Mmm," I said.

"I couldn't help but overhear what Ross said about the quintet. They're good but relatively new. Not many people have heard of them.

I've been wanting to hear them perform."

"Mmm."

"It's so cool that Ross gave you these roses."

"They make me sneeze," I said ungraciously. How could Ross have known that?

"He didn't know," Anna argued. "It was a sweet thing to do. I think he's trying to convince you to go to the dance, don't you?"

"It didn't work." I was feeling increasingly cross. Guilty, angry, and cross.

"Oh, Abby!" Anna cried.

"Oh, Anna," I said meanly. I opened my door, went in, and closed it behind me.

I sat down at my desk. I stared at my homework. One and one is two, I thought. But Ross and I are never going to add up. I knew it as surely as I knew anything.

But how could I convince Ross — and all the rest of the world — to believe me?

If I'd been rude to Ross, he hadn't noticed. I realized that the next morning as I approached my locker. I slowed down as I neared it, then stopped. At the base of the locker, wrapped in fancy florist's paper and tied with a ribbon, was a big red carnation.

It made my locker look like a big gray tombstone with a flower at the foot of it.

Students passing by were glancing down at it and then up at me. I bent and picked up the carnation. Attached to it I found a folded square of paper.

I opened it and read:

Although she cannot the sound of music hear,
Her name is music unto mine ear.
And if roses make her sneeze,
Perhaps this carnation will then please.
For Abby and the flowers are one,
But she's the fairest flower under the sun.

It was unsigned, and a good thing. Ross was *not* a poet, but he sure didn't know it.

I looked up and down the hall. My nose tickled and I sneezed. Then I opened the door and stuffed the flower and the poem inside. I was just lucky that none of my friends — or Anna — had come by before I'd had time to hide the flower and the poem.

The situation went from bad to worse in English class.

Walking into the room was like walking onto a stage. I was the unwilling star, and Ross was the audience of one. He kept staring at me and once, when he caught my eye, he smiled.

I didn't roll my eyes, so you can't really say I was rude.

Naturally, the discussion was about poetry again. But this time, I was prepared. When Ms. Colley asked for someone to read, I raised my hand. "I have a sonnet," I said. "Shakespeare. Number One Hundred and Thirty."

I'd gotten the idea from an old episode of *My So-Called Life* I'd just seen on television. The teacher had read this poem to the class.

I opened the book. I read:

" 'My mistress' eyes are nothing like the sun;
Coral is far more red than her lips' red;
If snow be white, why then her breasts are dun;
If hairs be wires, black wires grow on her head.
I have seen roses damasked, red and white,
But no such roses see I in her cheeks;
And in some perfumes is there more delight
Than in the breath that from my mistress reeks.
I love to hear her speak; yet well I know
That music hath a far more pleasing sound.
I grant I never saw a goddess go:
My mistress, when she walks, treads on the ground.
      And yet, by heaven, I think my love as rare
      As any she belied with false compare.' "

If I'd expected to catch Ms. Colley off guard, I didn't. She chuckled when I finished and said, "Yes. Good old One-thirty. Not what everyone expects from Will, is it? Well, what does that poem say, class? Anyone?"

Stunned silence. It was kind of blissful.

Then Ross's hand shot up. "It's about true love," he said.

"It's about reality," I retorted.

"It's about loving someone no matter what. Letting someone be herself, giving her a chance," he insisted.

"No way!" How had he gotten "give me a chance" from a poem like this?

I wanted to scream. I wanted to bean him with a book of poems. A *big* book of poems.

Ms. Colley intervened and steered the conversation back to the poem.

I refused to look at Ross, and I made sure that I was the first one out the door after class. I didn't want to discuss poetry, classical music, or flowers with him. I didn't want him around.

I did *not* want a BF right now. And even if I did (which I DID NOT) he wasn't my type, not now, not ever. Classical music and poetry? No and no. Maybe someone like Anna enjoyed that sort of thing but . . .

Hey, wait a minute, I thought. Anna. *Anna.*

Suddenly, just like that, I had pinpointed Ross's problem: He had fallen for the wrong twin.

Anna liked him. I was sure of that. Maybe I could convince Ross to shift his attentions to her.

But how? Too bad there weren't any sonnets dealing with *that*.

CHAPTER 9

Tuesday

I cant beleve Scout is leeving in fore days. Just fore days. Shes groan up to fast. Ill miss her. But not as bad as Andrew will. Its a good thing you warnd us, Mary Anne. So I was a little bit prepared.

With Kristy at the dentist and Nannie elbow-deep in cooking for her catering business, the Brewer-Thomas bunch needed a baby-sitter on Tuesday afternoon, and Claudia was it.

She went prepared, thanks to Mary Anne's description of her last sitting job and the discussion Kristy and I had had at the BSC meeting about what Andrew had said on Saturday.

No, she didn't take a new pet for Andrew (although we'd discussed future pet ideas for him) and no, she didn't fall back on her Kid-Kit. She brought along a book about a guide dog.

Since the weather was cold and miserable, outside activities were not a possibility. Nannie had promised treats from her kitchen in a little while, so Claudia wisely decided to steer clear of cookie baking.

That was fine with Karen. She wanted to make mice.

So did David Michael.

Claudia wasn't sure she heard correctly when, as she walked into the family room, Karen rose up from a litter of scraps of material and spools of thread and said, "Oh, good! You're here. You can help us make mice. These scissors won't cut and Nannie said we couldn't use her pinking shears unless you were here."

"I sure did," said Nannie, who had escorted

Claudia to the family room. She produced the pinking shears from her apron. They were big scissors with sharp, interlocking teeth that cut in a zigzag pattern. The zigzag cut helps keep material from unraveling.

"I'm going to cut up mice?" Claudia said in mock surprise as Nannie patted her shoulder, then headed back to the kitchen. (Believe me, I was as surprised as Claudia, when she told me about it later.)

"No!" That was Andrew.

"Yes," said Karen. She paused dramatically and exchanged a look with David Michael, then giggled and said, "Catnip mice. Will you draw us a pattern?"

"Slow down," said Claudia.

"I want to make something for Scout," put in Andrew.

"Dogs don't like catnip. Shannon doesn't, anyway," David Michael said, glancing at Shannon, who was lying on the rug near the door with Scout.

Claudia was beginning to get the picture. "You're making a catnip mouse toy for Pumpkin."

"Yes." Karen pointed at a small container on the windowsill. "That's the catnip. We're going to cut out mice, stuff them with catnip — "

"Mice with catnip *guts*," interrupted David Michael with relish.

"— and give them to Pumpkin. Maybe we'll make one for Mary Anne and Tigger too," Karen went on.

"Sounds good," said Claudia. She took a book and a piece of blank paper from a table and sat down next to the pile of scraps. "You and David Michael and Andrew pick out the best material for the mice, while I draw a mouse pattern."

Soon Claudia had helped to cut several "mice" out of felt and denim. She had just finished showing Karen and David Michael how they needed to sew the two sides of the mice together, leaving an opening, so that they could turn the mice inside out and then fill them with catnip "guts," when Andrew stood up. "Come on, Scout, let's go do something *fun*."

"This is fun," Karen said, frowning ferociously as she stitched her mouse together.

David Michael didn't say anything. He was concentrating too hard on the art of sewing a denim mouse.

"Where are you going?" Claudia asked Andrew.

"To my room, with my dog," Andrew replied.

Claudia helped David Michael and Karen finish one mouse each and waited until they had started on seconds before she excused herself to check on Andrew.

When Claudia opened the door to Andrew's room, he spun around and tried to shove a small, half-packed suitcase under the bed. She noticed that his piggy bank was upended on the bedside table. Scout was sitting on the bed, watching.

"Scout's not supposed to be on the bed, Andrew," Claudia said. "You know that."

"Scout's my dog and she can sit on my bed," Andrew argued.

"Scout isn't your dog, Andrew," Claudia replied. "Scout, off," she commanded. Scout jumped off the bed. Claudia, who actually thought the chocolate Lab looked a tad relieved, sat down where Scout had been sitting.

Andrew straightened up to scowl at her. Taking in more of the room, Claudia saw that drawers were open and clothes were spilling out.

"Packing for a trip?" Claudia asked innocently.

His face reddening, Andrew said, "No!"

"That's what it looks like." Claudia drew a deep breath and took a not-so-wild guess. "Maybe you and Scout are going somewhere."

Andrew's face grew even redder. "How did you know?" Then without waiting for Claudia to answer he said, "We're leaving, Scout and me. I'm not letting anyone take her away from me."

"Oh, Andrew." Claudia reached out and pulled the reluctant Andrew closer. She patted the bed next to her and he sat down. Scout laid her head on Andrew's knee, and he began to pet her.

"Scout likes me best," Andrew said, giving Claudia a defiant look.

"I can tell Scout likes you," Claudia said. "And you love Scout. She's your good friend."

Andrew nodded.

After a moment, Claudia said, "You've been lucky that Scout could live with you until she grew up enough to learn to be a guide dog. And you've done a really good job."

"You think so?" Andrew asked.

"I know it. When Scout goes to school, I believe she will be the best dog in her class. And when she graduates, someone who wants her very badly, and who needs a dog to be a friend and a guide, will be so happy to be partners with Scout."

Andrew hung his head. "But she'll be gone. She won't be mine anymore."

"She'll always be yours a little bit, Andrew. She'll never forget you, just as you'll never forget her."

"When Scout leaves, I won't have a big pet of my own. Karen has Pumpkin and David Michael has Shannon, but I don't have a dog or a cat," Andrew said. His voice sounded shaky.

"That's hard," Claudia said sympathetically. "It would make me sad."

He nodded. They sat in silence for a few minutes. Then Claudia said, "I brought a book about a dog that works as a guide dog. Maybe you'd like me to read it to you. And to Scout, of course."

Andrew nodded again. Claudia stood up and reached out to him. Hand in hand they went back to the family room, with Scout padding after them. Andrew sat on the sofa, leaning against Claudia, with Scout at his feet, while Claudia read, and Karen and David Michael made catnip mice.

She hoped she'd helped, but she couldn't be sure. Although she wished she could do something to make Andrew less sad, she couldn't think of a thing. Scout was leaving in four days. No matter what, it was going to be hard on the whole family, but especially on Andrew.

CHAPTER 10

"Roses and carnations! Abby, that's so sweet," said Stacey.

"It was one carnation, the roses made me sneeze, and what part of 'no' does Ross not understand?" I retorted.

We were at the Wednesday afternoon meeting of the BSC, which had quickly turned into some kind of "Support Ross as Abby's Date to the Dance" rally.

"It's nice that someone likes you," said Jessi.

"No, it's not. Not if you don't like him back," I said.

"But I thought you liked Ross," Claudia said.

"As a friend. But he's using up my friendship tolerance. Fast," I explained.

"Too bad he can't take the hint," said Kristy. "Now he's not going to have a dance date *and* he's going to lose a friend. A potential great friend."

I gave Kristy a grateful look.

"Didn't you like the book of *New Yorker* cartoons?" Stacey asked.

"Those I liked," I admitted. The book had been waiting for me at my locker on Tuesday morning. I had to admit, it had been funny — and a *lot* more interesting than my first couple of classes.

"I thought you would." Stacey looked smug.

I gave her a puzzled look.

Stacey said, "When Ross asked me, I told him you'd go for the cartoons. I said —"

"Wait a minute," I interrupted. "What are you saying? Are you saying that you gave Ross *advice*? When you KNOW I'M NOT INTERESTED?"

Yes, my voice was that loud. Mary Anne winced, and even Kristy looked taken aback.

Stacey stayed cool, though. "He asked. I was just trying to help."

"Help who?" Kristy snapped. "Not Abby, that's for sure."

Stacey opened her mouth, then closed it, looking angry.

Claudia took the opportunity to jump in. "I can see how it would be a little overwhelming, Abby. I mean, since you've never, well, had a boyfriend before."

Gritting my teeth, I said, "A, Don't patronize me. B, I've had a boyfriend, just not in Stoneybrook. I've had plenty of them. I mean, Long

Island is filled with my former boyfriends, okay?" (I was exaggerating, but I was *angry*.) "And C, I would never, ever, ever go out with someone just for the sake of going out with someone. I'll never be that desperate and dishonest."

That rocked Claudia's world. She sat back, her eyes widening. Stacey said with tight lips, "What are you implying? That we just date people for the sake of dating them?"

"If the shoe fits," I began.

Jessi intervened. "Stop it."

Mary Anne said at the same moment, "There are other reasons to go out with Ross."

"I'm talking, but no one's listening," I said to the wall. "I will not go out with Ross for *any* reason."

"So, what do you think, Claudia? Do you think Andrew will be able to handle Scout leaving?" Jessi said.

It was such a random question that we all stopped talking and looked at her. At that moment, Claudia's mother called, "Charlie's here."

Glancing at the clock, I saw that it read 6:01. Sounding as relieved as I felt, Kristy declared, "This meeting of the BSC is adjourned."

Kristy and I left without saying another word.

As we walked to the car, I said, "I guess I've

made Stacey and Claudia and Mary Anne pretty mad."

"Mary Anne's not mad. I think her feelings are probably hurt," Kristy observed. "But then, they made you mad too."

"True," I said.

"I guess we all need some space," Kristy said. She slammed the car door behind her. I leaned forward as Charlie started the engine.

"Charlie," I said, "you're a guy, right?"

"Yes," said Charlie as Kristy grinned.

"So give me some good guy advice."

"It's okay to invite him to do . . . whatever it is you want to invite him to do. He's waiting for you to call. Guys like that," Charlie said, jumping to the wrong conclusion before I said another word.

Kristy gave a hoot. "How would you know? Who's ever called you?"

"Plenty of girls," Charlie said. "That's why I'm the expert."

"That's *not* the problem," I said. I described what had been going on with Ross. "He doesn't get it," I concluded. "He thinks if I give him a chance, I'll change my mind. But I won't."

"Sounds like he's got it bad," Charlie said. "Poor guy."

"Don't you start," Kristy threatened him.

"No, I just mean, it's no fun to fall for someone and find out they won't fall for you, despite your considerable charms."

"Puh-lease." Kristy groaned.

Ignoring Kristy, Charlie continued, "But the worst thing you could do is to give him any hope at all. What you have to do is explain that it's a lost cause. That you will not now, or ever, date him. Make the situation plain. And don't take any more gifts from him. Give them back. That'll help get the point across. Plus, it'll hit him in the wallet, which is a great way to get someone's attention."

"That's it?" I said.

"That's it," Charlie said. "Simple. Easy."

Simple, maybe, but easy? No.

I only wished it were. Still, I was glad to know that Charlie thought I was doing the right thing.

As if I hadn't had enough Ross torment that day, the first word Anna said to me when I walked in the door was, "Ross —"

Before she could go on, I held up my hand. "No," I said. "No Ross. I'm declaring this house a Ross-free zone."

"But all I was going to say was that I bumped into him in the hall, and he seemed so nice. Maybe if you went to the dance, just gave him a chance —"

"If you like Ross so much, why don't *you* go to the dance with him?" I interrupted her.

That stopped Anna. When she did speak, I could tell I'd ruffled her feelings too. She shook her head. "That's not an option. He asked you, not me," she said almost sadly. "He wants to go out with you."

"Not necessarily. . . . Not the real me . . . not . . ."

But Anna was walking away, still shaking her head.

It was at that moment that an idea, equal in brilliance to one of Kristy's Great Ideas, began to take shape in my brain.

CHAPTER 11

So this was the plan. Anna liked Ross. Ross liked me. But he didn't really like *me*, because he didn't know me. And since he liked classical music and talking to Anna (and was much better at talking to Anna than talking to me), all I had to do was bring them together and make Ross see that it was really Anna he liked.

How was I going to do that? By being sneaky.

At school on Thursday, I lingered at my desk after English class. Ross stopped by. "Hi, Abby," he said.

"Hi, Ross." I gathered up my books. "Looks as if Ms. Colley is getting over her romance with the sonnet, doesn't it?"

"I guess."

"Anyway, I was wondering," I went on as we strolled out into the hall, "if maybe you could come by my house this afternoon. I think we need to talk."

Ross's eyes lit up. "This afternoon? Sure. No problem. What time?"

"Five-thirty? Is that too late?"

"No. Five-thirty. Perfect."

"See you then," I said, making my escape.

"Yes. Right. See you later, Abby." He said my name with a look that might have melted some people. Not me. But if I could just get him to say Anna's name like that, then, as Shakespeare said . . . "all's well that end's well."

When I caught up with Kristy and explained the plan to her, she was clearly impressed. "It could work," she said.

"Could? It better work," I answered. "Now, be sure and call me at five-forty, okay? You have to call on time. Otherwise it could turn messy."

"Am I a person with a reputation for being late?" Kristy asked. "I think not."

"Good," I said.

I had lined up Ross and Kristy. Now all I had to do was convince Anna to go along with the plan.

I'm sure you've guessed what it is. The old "leave them alone together" ploy. Ross would arrive, Anna and I would both talk to him, the phone would ring, I'd talk to Kristy for a nice *long* time, and when I returned, Ross would have realized who his one true love really was.

I just hoped Anna would agree.

At first, she didn't. "Abigail Stevenson, are you completely out of your mind?" she cried.

"No. Not yet. But Ross is sending me dangerously close to the edge."

"I won't do it."

"Come on, Anna. All you have to do is talk to him. What's the big deal? And if you like him and he likes you, who's crazy?"

Anna thought about that for a moment. A little smile curved her lips. "Ross *is* nice," she said.

"He is, he is," I agreed, then added hastily, "for you. Not for me."

"Okay. What's the worst that could happen?"

"Good," I said. And mentally I added, "Good-bye, Ross." If, after he'd spent a little time with Anna, he still hadn't seen the error of his ways, I would give him the straightforward go-away talk Charlie had suggested. That would finish it.

I was *so* right about Anna liking Ross. The closer 5:30 came, the more nervous she grew. She tore through her closet, trying on one outfit after another. She hated everything. Her hair was a mess (according to Anna). As Ross's estimated time of arrival approached, I finally unbuttoned the shirt I'd been wearing. "Here," I said. "Wear this. It's my absolute favorite good-luck shirt."

Anna had just finished buttoning it up when the doorbell rang. I grabbed Anna's sweater and pulled it over my head. As I did, I somehow managed to poke myself in the eye. When I finished blinking, I realized I'd torn a contact.

The doorbell rang again.

"Abby!" wailed Anna.

"I can handle it. Stay calm," I ordered. I raced into the bathroom, ditched my contacts, grabbed my glasses, and threw open the door just as the bell rang a third time. "Ross!" I gasped.

"Hi," said Ross.

"Come on in." I stepped back and saw that he had brought flowers. I couldn't identify them. And I didn't want them. I was just about to tell him to take the flowers away, as Charlie had instructed, when Ross stepped past me, his smile widening. He held the flowers out — to Anna, as she came into the hall. "For you."

Anna said, "Oh!"

Ross continued, "I love that shirt. You always look great in it."

He'd given the flowers to Anna. I, Abby, was no longer the object of Ross's affections!

Then his last comment sank in, and my heart sank with it.

He thought Anna was me.

Anna was leading Ross toward the kitchen,

her face buried in the flowers. "Narcissus," she said. "Where did you find these, in the middle of winter?"

"My mom knows how to make bulbs bloom out of season," Ross said. "Don't forget, she's a florist."

"A florist. Your house must be full of flowers."

"Year-round."

I was willing myself not to sneeze. "Why don't we go to the family room?" I suggested.

Ross looked surprised. Anna said, "Okay."

Then, right on cue, the phone rang.

"It's for me," I said.

Now Ross looked even more surprised. "I'm expecting a call," I explained. "That's how I know."

But already his attention had shifted back to Anna. As they walked out, I heard him say, "The shirt makes your eyes look different. I'm glad these flowers didn't make you sneeze."

"But," Anna said and stopped. She glanced over her shoulder at me. Now she had figured it out too.

The phone rang a third time as Anna disappeared with Ross.

I snatched up the phone, closed the kitchen door, and whispered, "Mayday! Mayday!"

Kristy said, "Abby?"

"The worst has happened," I told her. "Ross has us mixed up. He thinks Anna is me!"

For once in my life, I wasn't trying to be funny, but Kristy gave a shout of laughter. "No way."

"I'm telling the truth. Kristy, what am I going to do?"

Kristy stopped laughing. "Wow," she said. "This is a spin I didn't expect."

"No kidding. So how do I unspin it?"

"I don't know." Kristy thought for a moment and then said, "Why don't you just see how things go? You know, join them and . . . just see."

"That's the best you can do? That does not even register on the Great Idea scale," I said.

"I don't hear any better ideas from you."

Kristy was right. "Okay," I said. "But keep thinking. If you come up with anything, call me *immediately*.

"I will," Kristy promised.

After I hung up the phone, I stayed in the kitchen awhile longer. Part of it was cowardice, and part of it was to give Ross and Anna more quality time together. I figured that the better Ross liked Anna, the less likely he was to be upset by the little mix-up that had just occurred.

They were in the middle of an intense discussion about music when I walked back into the family room. They were sitting on the couch, leaning toward each other, totally engrossed in the conversation.

"Hi," I interrupted. "Having a classical moment?"

"Uh," said Ross, "yeah."

"Great. I just wondered if you would like anything to eat or drink," I said.

Anna answered. She said, "No thank you, *Anna*."

So Anna hadn't told Ross who she was.

"Are you sure, *Abby*?" I asked.

Her eyes met mine. She nodded. She was sure about the masquerade, even if I wasn't.

I heard the back door open. Then Mom called, "Hello? I'm home!"

Anna and I panicked. Mom could tell us apart — and she would give us away. I turned and hurried out to stop her.

Ross said, "I'm kind of thirsty, actually. What do you have?"

"Water," I said. I heard Mom open the hall closet and take off her coat. "Uh, orange juice. Soda. Diet soda . . . milk." The door to the hall closet closed. "Apple juice?"

"Apple juice sounds good."

"It's on its way," I said, and tried to make a quick exit. I nearly bowled Mom over.

"Abby!" she said. "What's the rush? And why are you wearing your glasses? I thought they drove you crazy in the cold weather."

Behind me I heard Ross say just one word: "Abby?"

CHAPTER 12

"Hi, Mom," I said. "This is Ross. He goes to school with me and . . . with us. Ross, this is our mom."

"Hello, Ross," Mom said.

"Hello," Ross managed to say, but his eyes darted between me and Anna.

Anna looked as if she felt a little sick. Ross stood up.

"I'm going to have a cup of tea and unwind a little," Mom told us. "Can I fix anybody anything?"

"I was about to bring Ross some apple juice," I said.

"No. Thanks. I changed my mind," Ross sputtered. He began walking toward the door. "Nice to meet you, Mrs. Stevenson."

"Nice to meet you, Ross," said Mom with a quizzical look at Anna and me.

Mom left and Ross said, "Could I use the

phone? I have to call my brother to come pick me up."

"I'll get it for you," I said, and raced out of the room.

But if I hoped giving Anna and Ross a few more minutes alone would help matters, I was extremely wrong. When I returned with the phone, Anna looked miserable and so did Ross. They were both staring at the floor.

Ross made his call. As he hung up, he said, "He'll be here in a minute. He has a job after school delivering flowers for Mom's shop, and he's in the neighborhood."

I took the phone from Ross and said, "Ross. About what just happened."

"Pretty funny," said Ross. "Ha-ha." He was being very sarcastic.

"Ohhh," said Anna. "Ross, it's not what you think. It was an accident!"

"My coat?" said Ross.

He followed me to the hall closet, reached for his coat, and put it on.

"Ross, I'm sorry," I said.

"I think I hear my brother," he answered.

He opened the front door and walked out.

Anna turned to me, and her eyes actually filled with tears. "Thanks for *nothing*, Abby. I hope someday I can repay you with a plan that is just as stupid!"

"Hey, you were part of it too. You pretended to be me, don't forget!"

Anna said, "What was I supposed to do? You closed the kitchen door and left me standing there with him!"

"You could have told him then."

"I couldn't! He'd think we did it on purpose and then he'd hate me forever. And he did, and he does!"

"No, he hates *me*. I'll explain it to him and he'll see that it's all my fault." I couldn't stand the hurt look on my sister's face. "It'll be all right, Anna, I promise."

"Ha!" Anna shouted. She turned and stormed out of the room. A few minutes later, I heard the door to her room slam and then the violin music start. I didn't recognize it, but even as a tone-deaf person, I could tell that it was not a soothing tune she was playing.

I started to go into the kitchen to see if I could talk to Mom about what had happened. Then I thought about how I'd managed to make everyone I knew angry lately, except for maybe Kristy and possibly Jessi, and decided against it. The best way to end this day, I decided, was to keep a low profile.

As to how I was going to survive the next day, I didn't even want to think about it.

*   *   *

Friday at last, and the last day of Valentine's Day madness. The dance, and Valentine's Day itself, were on Saturday. This would have been a cause for me to rejoice, ordinarily. But not this Friday, not this Valentine's Day Dance eve.

The good news was that at breakfast, Anna spoke to me. She said, as I came into the kitchen and she stood up from the table, "I'm going to apologize to Ross today. I think you should too."

"Good idea," I said. "I'll do it first thing."

Anna nodded. Mom came into the kitchen. Anna left. I sighed.

It was going to be a long, long day.

My locker was flower free when I arrived, but I noticed that more than one locker around me had valentine-type envelopes wedged between the door and the frame or stuck in the locker vent. And I saw one bouquet of flowers resting against another locker nearby. The tombstone effect didn't bother me so much today. I was feeling a little grave.

My joke cheered me up. I wasn't beaten yet, I decided, and went in search of Ross to apologize. As I wandered the halls, I was relieved that no one asked me about the inadvertent twin switch Anna and I had pulled the previous evening. Either Ross hadn't had time to tell anyone, or he wasn't going to talk about it. I fervently hoped it was the second choice.

I found Ross near his homeroom. He turned as I approached him. I smiled, opened my mouth to begin my apology, and . . . he walked right by me.

I stood there with my mouth open, feeling foolish. The final bell snapped me out of it, and I went to class. I guess I don't have to add that Ross ignored me in English. Pointedly.

I don't know whether everyone else in the BSC ignored me at lunch, because I didn't join them at our usual table. I took refuge in the library, where I stared at the same page in my history book for the entire lunch hour.

I made sure that I was home from a nice, long run in time to catch a ride with Kristy when Charlie took her to the BSC meeting. No way was I going to walk in there alone. I didn't want Charlie to know what had happened, or that I had not followed his excellent advice and as a result was the local pariah. So I kept quiet. Kristy started to ask me about what happened, but I gestured to her that we'd talk later.

We were a little early, but everyone else had already assembled.

"Hi," said Kristy. She checked her watch, glanced at Claudia's clock, and raised her eyebrows. For once, she wasn't going to be able to give the near-tardy members her warning look.

Everyone sort of mumbled a greeting. I said hello to my feet and sat down quickly in the corner.

A flurry of phone calls kept us distracted at first, and I was glad for that.

After Mary Anne had entered the last appointment in the record book and Kristy had called our client back to confirm it, silence fell. Claudia rooted around in a bag of bite-size Snickers, extracted one, and held out the bag. "Candy, anyone?"

No one wanted any. Silence.

"It's been cold," Jessi said.

"Yeah," agreed Mary Anne. "But at least it hasn't snowed or sleeted anymore."

"I just hope it stays that way through the weekend," Stacey said. "Nice, I mean."

"It would be too bad if we had a blizzard or something on Saturday night . . ." Mary Anne stopped. Her voice trailed off.

Saturday night was the night of the dance, of course.

Although I'm the newest member of the BSC, I've been around long enough to know that at any other meeting that occurred the night before a dance, the talk would center almost exclusively on the dance: who was wearing what, who was going with whom, what the decorations would be, who the DJ would be, and so on.

But no one wanted to mention the dance, because who knew what would happen? And that wasn't fair. Just because I'd declared my life a dance-free zone at the moment didn't mean that my friends had to follow suit.

So I took a deep breath and said, "About the dance."

I definitely had my audience's attention.

"Sorry," I said. "I'm sorry I snapped at all of you at the last meeting. I'm sorry I implied that you would date anyone just for the sake of going on a date. I'm sorry — "

"I'm sorry too," Mary Anne cut in. "I didn't mean to make you feel as if having a date to the dance was so . . . earthshakingly important."

Stacey nodded. "And it was wrong of me not to listen to you, Abby. You told me you weren't interested in Ross, but I just ignored it because *I* wanted you to be at the dance — no matter what you wanted. I should have listened to what you said. You had a right to be angry."

"You did, Abby," Claudia agreed. "I accept your apology and I apologize too."

We all fell silent again, but this time, the silence was much more comfortable.

"Well," Kristy said at last, in a hearty voice, "I'm glad we can agree that having a boyfriend, or not having one, isn't worth ruining a friendship over."

I grinned. Trust Kristy to sledgehammer a point home.

Looking around, I realized we were all grinning.

I held up my hands. "Okay, okay," I said. "Talk. Who's wearing what to the dance?"

Jessi said, "Well, I'm going with some other kids from my grade, and we all want to wear red. I've got this red shirt that would look terrific, but maybe it's a little too, you know, dressy."

"I know the shirt you're talking about," Claudia said instantly. "It'll look great with the right accessories."

My eyes met Kristy's. She made a face. I shook my head and leaned back. I was on track with my friends again, and that was a pretty good valentine for me.

CHAPTER 13

I came home from the BSC meeting feeling better. I actually felt like singing. I warmed up with an off-key medley of Aretha Franklin tunes while I organized dinner.

Anna set the table in silent mode. I tossed the salad and watched her out of the corner of my eye, singing little bits of "Respect" (one of my favorites). Normally, anything resembling an attempt at a song from my lips makes Anna wince. Sometimes, if I sing loudly and long enough, I can make her beg me to stop.

Now, I couldn't even get her to wince. I gave up. I quit singing.

Anna sighed. Then she said (apparently to the handful of silverware she was holding), "Did you apologize to Ross?"

"I tried," I said. "He wasn't interested. He wouldn't even give me a chance."

Laying each knife, fork, and spoon in its place with care, Anna said, "I tried to talk to him too. He just walked on by. He acted as if I didn't exist. I thought maybe if you talked to him, since he likes you . . ."

"Not anymore he doesn't." I didn't add that this, at least, was a relief. I sensed that levity would not be acceptable.

"Maybe you didn't try hard enough," Anna said.

"I tried," I insisted. "Believe me."

"He never liked me. Now . . ." Again Anna let her voice trail off.

Naturally, Mom noticed the atmosphere of doom and gloom at dinner. After several attempts to carry on a conversation with Anna and me, she said, "Okay, you two, tell me what's going on."

"Ross," Anna blurted out miserably.

"That boy I met yesterday afternoon?"

We both nodded. We hadn't told Mom the whole story the night before, just that Ross had stopped by and had gotten us mixed up. Since Mom had seen us play the old twin-switch routine on other friends, she hadn't thought too much of it. And since she had brought work home from her office and spent most of dinner flipping through the pages of a report, she hadn't noticed that Anna and I were not in our peak conversational form.

But that was the night before. Tonight, without anything to distract her, how could she not notice?

"What about Ross?" Mom inquired.

"He was really upset when he discovered we'd pulled the twin swap on him," I explained. I paused, took a deep breath, and told Mom the whole story of Ross's Unrequited Love.

When I'd finished, Mom said, "Well, that's quite a story. And quite a problem."

"How do we solve it?" Anna asked.

"I don't know." Mom shook her head. "You may just have to wait and hope that time will help Ross's hurt feelings."

Anna sighed. "I was thinking of writing him a note, but I don't think he would read it."

"Notes are bad," I said. "What if your note fell into the wrong hands?"

I didn't want what had happened to spread all over SMS.

Anna didn't either. She understood what I meant immediately. "You're right," she said.

"Maybe we could convince someone else to talk to Ross," I said. "He might listen to an apology from us if someone else talked to him first."

"Who?" Anna asked. "And what if it made him even more upset that we had told someone else what we did?"

This was also a problem.

We cleared the table and loaded the dishwasher, and then Anna and I sat back down while Mom made a cup of hot tea. I stared hard at Anna. My twin. *Double the trouble, double the fun*, my mind sang, skipping in and out of old advertising jingles and clichés. Two for the price of one.

"That's it!" I said aloud.

"What?"

"Two of us. If we apologize together, maybe Ross will listen. Especially if we talk to him at his house. I mean, he can't duck into the boys' bathroom or stalk away down the hall at home, can he?"

"At his house? Go to his house?" Anna couldn't believe what I was saying.

"Yes. And the sooner the better." I bounced up. "Mom! I have an idea! Can you give us a ride somewhere?"

By the time we'd organized our expedition to Ross's, Anna had changed shirts twice. She wore her glasses. I wore my contact lenses.

When we pulled up in front of the Browns' house, Mom said, "I'll wait in the car with my tea. Good luck." She raised her travel mug in salute, then leaned back as we climbed out of the car and trooped up the walk to Ross's front door.

He was definitely surprised to see us. He

took a step back and said, "Abby? Anna?"

When Ross stepped back, Anna started backing up too. But I wouldn't let her. I put my hand on her arm and propelled her across the doorstep. I figured that once we were inside, he wouldn't throw us out.

"What are you doing here?" Ross asked.

We were inside now. I closed the door. Ross didn't resist. "We came to talk," I began. "But I don't think we should do that standing in the hall."

Anna still hadn't said a word.

Ross was silent for a moment, then said, "No one's in the living room. Come on."

We stood awkwardly for a moment, Ross glancing from me to Anna and back again. Then he smiled just a little. "Maybe you two should wear name tags, just so I don't make the same mistake and mix you up again."

He sat down. So I did too, on the sofa across from him. I pulled Anna down beside me.

Then I surprised Anna as well as Ross. "I've come to apologize to *both* of you," I said.

Anna finally spoke. "Abby!" she said.

"This whole mess is my fault," I continued.

"Abby," Anna interrupted, "wait."

I held up my hand. "No, listen. Ross, I like you. You're a great person and I'd be glad to be friends with you, but I don't want to go to the dance with you."

Ross ducked his head a little and his cheeks reddened. "I think I've got *that* figured out by now," he muttered.

"But maybe if I'd been a little more emphatic, made less of a joke of your invitation, you might have figured it out sooner," I said.

"Maybe I should have been listening," replied Ross, surprising me. "I guess I just didn't want to hear it."

"Okay," I said. I was more than willing to let him take some of the responsibility for that part of the mess, since what he had said was true. "Anyway, when I invited you over, it was for two reasons. I wanted to make clear how I felt, once and for all, and I wanted to try to make you see that Anna might be much more the sort of person you'd like than I am."

Now Anna ducked her head and blushed. I went on. "I never intended to play a twin-switch trick on you, and Anna certainly never did." I explained about the contact lens accident and the borrowed shirt. And how, once I realized Ross had made a mistake, I hadn't jumped in to correct it right away, because Ross was getting along so well with the right twin, even if it was by the wrong name.

"It was just one of those mistakes that grew bigger and bigger, and it's all my fault, and it's killing me that you two are so right for each other and might not ever figure it out because of what I did," I finished in a rush.

Silence. Whew. Then I realized that even if it was an awkward silence, it wasn't without possibilities. Anna was glancing at Ross from under her eyelashes. Ross kept looking up at her and then looking away. Both were seriously blushing.

"That was you talking, Anna," Ross said finally (to the rug). "You weren't pretending to like classical music or flowers to imitate Abby?"

"Are you kidding?" I answered. "I like soccer, not string quartets. The only flowers I like are the ones I mow down on a soccer field on the way to the goal. If I — "

"Abby," said Anna. "Be quiet."

So I was.

She looked at Ross steadily now. "It was me," she said. "Not Abby. And I'm sorry I didn't tell you then, when it all happened."

"Nah," said Ross, and he was looking directly at Anna now. "You don't have to apologize, Anna. It's okay."

"Great!" I jumped to my feet.

Ross and Anna stood up too. They were still looking at each other. Then Ross said, "So, Anna. You want to go hear the Stoneybrook String Quartet tomorrow afternoon at the community center?"

Anna's face was suddenly radiant. "I'd like that," she said. She added shyly, "Ross."

This time, I had sense enough to keep my mouth shut. But inside, I was cheering.

Ross hadn't invited Anna to the dance, but somehow, from the look on my sister's face, I knew that the Stoneybrook String Quartet invitation was at least as good.

It just might turn out to be a decent Valentine's Day after all.

CHAPTER 14

Saturday

Valentine's Day might be hearts and flowers to some people, but for our family, especially Andrew, it was a day of heartbreak. This was the day that Scout left us to begin her training to become a guide dog. Even though we've known that we'd have to say good-bye to her, somehow we'd managed not to think about it — or in Andrew's case, to believe it at all.

Kristy had had trouble sleeping. When she finally did fall asleep, it was early in the morning, and then she slept hard until the sound of the alarm clock almost blew her out of bed.

She stumbled around getting dressed and feeling disoriented and blue. She knew why she'd slept badly. Scout was leaving that day, and Kristy was going to miss her. Saying good-bye to Scout also reminded Kristy much too much of saying good-bye to Louie, the old collie who had been Kristy's best friend. Louie died not long ago, and Kristy still misses him.

But Scout wasn't dying, Kristy reminded herself as she went down to breakfast. She was just leaving home to start her new life, the one she was meant for.

Passing by the hall bathroom, Kristy was stopped by the sounds of a faucet running and water splashing. "Hold still!" she heard Karen command in what, for her, was a whisper.

Kristy knocked on the bathroom door and heard a *thump, thump, thump* in reply. Finally, David Michael's voice said, "Who is it?"

"Karen? David Michael?" Kristy said. "May I come in?"

Thump, thump, thump. Kristy identified the sound. It was a dog's tail hitting porcelain.

"Is Shannon in there with you?"

"It's Scout," said Karen. "You may come in."

Karen, David Michael, and Scout were all pretty wet, although Scout was the only one actually in the bathtub. "We're giving Scout a bath," Karen explained unnecessarily.

"We want her to look perfect when she gets to her school," David added.

Karen said, "Because it's not easy being a new kid at school. You want everything just right."

Kristy was touched. She looked down into Scout's intelligent, trusting brown eyes and felt a lump in her throat. "Good idea," she said. "Let me help you dry her off."

Several towels later, Scout emerged shining and beautiful from her bath. At that moment, the door burst open.

Everyone jumped except Scout. Her tail thumped hello against the toilet.

"What are you doing to my dog?" Andrew demanded.

"She's not your dog, Andrew," said Karen, her chin going up. "She's a guide dog in training. You know that."

"She IS NOT!" Andrew cried in a voice that put Karen's outdoor voice to shame. "Come here, Scout. Come on, girl."

Scout went obediently toward Andrew. Karen was about to protest, but Kristy stopped her. "You should give Shannon a bath too, don't you think?" Kristy suggested. "So she won't feel left out."

"You're right!" David Michael said.

"I'll get more towels," Karen volunteered instantly.

"I'll get Shannon," David Michael said.

Kristy mentally added a mop to the list, realizing that after two dog baths, the bathroom floor would be a small sea.

But in the meantime, she had to have breakfast. A little damp and doggy, Kristy made her way to the breakfast table.

"Karen and David Michael are giving Shannon a bath," Kristy informed her family. "Scout just had one."

"Poor Andrew is taking Scout's departure so hard," said Kristy's mom. "But then, so am I."

"We all are," said Nannie.

Emily Michelle, in her high chair, didn't say anything. She just banged her spoon on the tray.

Watson looked at his watch. "It'll be time to start soon," he said. Kristy's mom nodded. She and Watson were taking Scout to the Guide Dog Foundation on Long Island. They had to take the ferry, and it would be a long trip.

Suddenly, Kristy wasn't hungry anymore, maybe because of the "good-bye, Scout" lump in her throat. *But it's not as if I will never see*

Scout again, she argued silently with herself. She knew that after a year, if Scout's new person agreed and if Scout were living close enough, they could visit her.

But it wouldn't be the same, and Kristy knew it.

She stood up. "I think I'll go see how Andrew is doing," she said.

Considerably more splashing was coming from the upstairs bathroom as Kristy walked by again, and she couldn't help but smile to herself. Shannon wasn't taking to her bath as patiently as Scout had.

Kristy found the door to Andrew's room closed. She knocked.

"Go away," Andrew grumbled.

"I don't want to," Kristy said simply. "Will you let me in?"

She put her hand on the doorknob and found it locked.

"You can't come in," said Andrew. "And we're not coming out. Not until it is too late to take Scout away from me."

That stumped Kristy for a minute. She knew that Watson would be able to jiggle the door open pretty quickly, but she didn't think that would be the best solution.

"Andrew," she said, "why do you want Scout to be a failure?"

"She's not a failure!" Andrew shouted.

"But she will be if you keep her locked in with you. She won't go to school and then she'll be a failure. And Scout's a smart dog. She'll know."

"But she's my dog," said Andrew.

"No, she's not your dog. She belongs to somebody who needs her. She belongs to someone who can't see, someone who is waiting for her to go through her training, and help that person walk through the world without being afraid."

It was a long speech. Was Andrew still listening?

"Andrew? Let me in, please," Kristy said. "I promise I won't let Scout out."

After what seemed like an endless wait, Kristy heard the lock click and saw the doorknob turn. Andrew stepped back. Scout was on the floor by Andrew's bed. "Scout, stay," Andrew said, although Scout didn't look as if she were going anywhere. "Come in," he said to Kristy.

Kristy walked in and sat down on one side of the chocolate Lab. She began to stroke Scout's soft fur. *Thump, thump, thump* went Scout's tail.

Andrew sat down on the other side of Scout and put his hand on her collar possessively.

Kristy closed her eyes and leaned back.

"What're you doing?" Andrew asked.

"I'm pretending I'm blind and I'm waiting to meet my new dog. I've heard all about her — that her name is Scout and that she's beautiful."

"And smart," Andrew added.

"I'm worried about Scout, though," Kristy continued. "I know that she had a wonderful family to raise her when she was a puppy and that she had to leave them. I know she's had to adjust to a new home at the Guide Dog Foundation while she was in school, and I know it was lots and lots of hard work."

"School *is* hard," Andrew agreed.

"But I've been told how smart Scout is, and how hard her puppy-walker family worked to teach her all the right things, and how hard Scout herself worked in school to be a good guide dog."

Kristy paused. Andrew was silent.

"I've decided I'm going to give Scout the best home in the world, because I already love her. I'm going to show her how much she means to me, how glad I am that she is coming to live with me to help me get around."

Kristy opened her eyes. "But Scout can't do all of that if you don't let her, Andrew."

Andrew bit his lip. He nodded slowly. "I know," he said. He released Scout's collar and began stroking her head. "Good girl," he murmured. "Good Scout."

"You have to tell Scout it's okay to go, Andrew," Kristy said. "It's very important."

Andrew nodded. "I know," he said again.

A knock sounded on the door. David Michael said, "Andrew, is Scout in there with you?"

Andrew put his arms around Scout's neck. "Yes," he mumbled into her fur.

"Yes," said Kristy, so that David Michael could hear. To Andrew she asked, "Should I let him in?"

Andrew nodded, still holding Scout.

David Michael came in, followed by Shannon. He said, "It's almost time for Scout to go. We should take her downstairs."

Slowly, reluctantly, Andrew released his hold on Scout. "Be good," he said. He stood up and walked to the other side of his room.

As if she sensed Andrew's unhappiness, Shannon walked over to him and pushed her nose into one of his hands. Automatically, Andrew lifted his hand to Shannon's head and stroked it.

To Scout he said, "It's not so hard to go to a new home, Scout, if you like it. You'll like it. You'll see."

David Michael looked at his younger stepbrother. Then he looked down at Shannon. He said, "Shannon likes you a lot, Andrew, I can tell."

Andrew nodded mutely.

From downstairs, Karen called, "Scout! It's time!"

Hearing her name, Scout stood up.

Karen called again, "Scout, come!"

Without looking back, Scout trotted out of the room.

Tears welled in Andrew's eyes.

David Michael looked as if he were about to cry too.

Then Andrew wailed, "My dog is go-o-o-one!"

Kristy, who was feeling more than a little choked up herself, knelt beside Andrew and put her arms around him. He began to cry noisily into her shoulder.

Then David Michael walked over to Andrew and began to pat him on the shoulder. "Don't cry, Andrew," he said. "Don't cry."

Andrew kept crying.

David Michael said, "You know what? Since Shannon likes you so much, you can share her with me. She can be your puppy too."

As if by magic, Andrew's wails stopped. He sniffled and looked at David Michael. "Re-ally?" he asked.

"Really?" Kristy echoed, surprised in spite of herself.

"Really," David Michael said. He folded his arms. "But it's a lot of hard work. You have to help walk her, and clean up the yard, and feed her, and keep fresh water in her bowl, you know."

"I know. Like with Scout," said Andrew.

At the mention of Scout's name, they all stopped talking. Then Kristy said, "I guess we'd better go wish Scout a safe trip."

Downstairs, Scout was already in her guide-dog-in-training vest, and her leash was on. Watson was taking her belongings to the car while Kristy's mom held the leash, and Karen and Emily Michelle petted Scout. Charlie and Sam were trying to act cool, but I could tell they were having trouble saying good-bye to Scout too. She sat and wagged her tail and smiled at everyone, her tongue lolling out. Scout didn't know she was leaving forever. To her it was just another ride in the car.

"We'll come visit you in a year," Karen promised. "Even if you're in Australia."

"I'd like to go to Australia," Nannie said. She scooped Emily Michelle onto one hip, then bent and stroked Scout's ears. "You've been an education and a joy," she said to Scout. "I'm glad I met you."

Andrew began to cry again. Karen, whose own eyes were suspiciously bright behind her glasses, held up her hand toward Andrew like a traffic cop. "Stop crying," she commanded. "You'll upset Scout."

And indeed, Scout was staring searchingly at Andrew. She stood up and walked forward and licked his cheeks as he struggled not to cry. " 'Bye, Scout," he said. Then he tore himself loose and flung himself against Kristy's leg. She put her arm across his shoulders.

Time had gone so fast, Kristy thought, staring at Scout. It seemed like only yesterday that Scout had been a roly-poly puppy, full of wiggly excitement and endless puppy love.

But she'd grown up. She was a dignified young dog now, sleek and beautiful and ready to begin her new life.

"Good-bye, Scout," said Kristy, and suddenly that was all she could say because of the lump in her throat.

" 'Bye, Scout," David Michael echoed, giving Scout a last hug. Then Shannon stepped forward and the two dogs touched noses. Was Shannon saying good-bye too? Kristy wondered. Did Shannon know? It sure looked that way.

Kristy's mom led Scout out the door for the last time. It closed behind them, and Scout was gone.

"I have to go find Pumpkin," Karen announced with sudden urgency. As she bustled past, Kristy saw the shining track of a tear on Karen's cheek.

David Michael said to Andrew, "Maybe we

should take Shannon in the backyard to play ball, so she won't miss Scout."

Andrew nodded and the three of them left too.

Nannie said, "I need to get to work."

Kristy reached out and took Emily Michelle. She walked to the window just as the car pulled out of the drive.

"Say 'bye-'bye to Scout," said Kristy.

" 'Bye-'bye," Emily Michelle said.

" 'Bye," Kristy echoed softly, and watched until the car, with Scout's noble head framed by the window, was out of sight.

CHAPTER 15

"My hair is having some kind of attack," Anna groaned.

"Your hair is fine," I assured her (for about the tenth time).

"Your sure this shirt is okay?"

"Perfect," I said.

"I don't know. . . ."

"You're a symphony," I told her. "An aria. A concerto."

"A marching band?" Anna asked, suddenly smiling. She looked great.

I smiled back. "Whatever. Ross is going to think you look fabuloso, because you do."

Just then, the doorbell rang.

Anna jumped and gave me a panicked look.

"No way am I answering that door," I said. I gave her a little push out of the room. "Go. Have fun."

I lingered at the top of the stairs as my sister went down to meet Ross for their date — if that's what it was — to hear the Stoneybrook String Quartet play. I'd half hoped he'd bring her flowers or a box of V-day candy, but he didn't. On the other hand, he did say, "Wow, you look terrific . . . Anna," when he saw her.

Anna laughed a little nervously. "I *am* Anna, and you look great too."

"Thanks," Ross said.

An awkward silence fell, then Ross said, "I guess we'd better go."

"I'm looking forward to hearing them play," Anna said. "I heard them at a Christmas concert, and I thought they were very good."

"Was that the concert at the Stoneybrook Day School auditorium? I was there too!"

The door closed behind them and I smiled to myself. Nervous or not, my sister and Ross had plenty in common. They wouldn't run out of things to say to each other.

I was right about that. By the time Anna and Ross returned from the concert, they were talking nonstop. When the front door closed and Anna came into the den, her eyes were shining.

"Was the music nice?" I asked.

"Never mind that," Anna said. "Abby! He asked me to the dance tonight."

"That's great, Anna." I jumped to my feet, flicked off the soccer game I was watching, and said, "We'd better get to work."

We spent most of the rest of the afternoon

going through both our closets, picking out just the right outfit. Needless to say, Anna was too nervous to eat much dinner.

"When I was dating your father," Mom teased Anna, "he would have been insulted if I'd picked at my food the way you're doing."

"But Dad was a great cook, Mom," Anna said.

I raised my eyebrows. "And I'm not?"

"The Queen of the Take-out Menu," Anna shot back. She wasn't too nervous to hold her own. "Besides, you're not eating anything either."

"I have big Valentine's Day plans myself," I said. "Kristy and I are going to a horror movie and then for pizza. We're going to see *Pepperoni Man*, the one about the delivery guy who — "

"I don't want to know," Anna protested.

"Very romantic," Mom said, amused.

"My kind of Valentine's Day," I told them.

The doorbell rang right on time. I gave my sister a hug and whispered, "Happy Valentine's Day. Have fun."

"I will," said Anna. "Definitely."

After Anna and Ross left for the dance, I grabbed a sweater and pulled it on, bundled myself into my coat, and headed for Kristy's house.

Kristy met me at the door. "Get me out of here," she said. "Both Charlie and Sam have dates tonight and they've only spent the last three hours in the bathroom, staring at themselves in the mirror." She wrinkled her nose. "And drowning themselves in cologne."

I laughed and told Kristy about Anna's big night out with Ross.

"Excellent," said Kristy.

Nannie gave us a ride downtown. In every drugstore window were enormous heart-shaped boxes of candy. One of the florists (not Ross's mom) had done their display window entirely in red flowers arranged into hearts.

"The candy will all be half price tomorrow," I pointed out. "Maybe we should pool our funds and make an investment for the next BSC meeting."

"A very worthy idea," Kristy said, reverting to her Madame President mode for a moment. Then she grinned. "And Claudia will love it."

We timed our arrival at the theater perfectly and snagged two seats in the dead middle (that's a joke, in case you didn't notice). We had just settled back and begun to make serious progress with the popcorn when the manager walked onto the stage.

He held up his hands. "I'd like for everyone to take out their ticket stubs, please."

I fished around in my pocket and found the stub.

"Does anyone have a ticket stub stamped

with a small red heart?" the manager asked.

I glanced down. "Oh."

"You?" Kristy said.

The manager continued. "If you do, please come to the front of the theater for a special prize."

I stood up. "It's me," I said.

People began to applaud, and a few whistled and hooted. I heard a familiar voice call, "Is it a soccer ball?" and turned to see a row of eighth-grade guys from SMS in the back — including Alan Gray, the most disgusting boy in the class. I made a face and walked to the front of the theater.

Beaming, the manager produced an enormous box of valentine chocolates. "Just a little something to help you celebrate Valentine's Day," he announced as my face turned bright red. "I hope you have someone special to share it with."

Alan and his cronies cheered loudly.

"I do," I managed to say to the manager, who looked pleased. "Thank you."

"Happy Valentine's Day," he said.

Alan and his friends were still cheering and being generally obnoxious as the lights went down and I sank into my seat. The box of chocolates was *huge* and incredibly gaudy.

Kristy was laughing so hard that I had to give her a Look.

"Sorry." She gasped. "But you should have seen your face."

"No one will ever believe this," I said. I noticed that the bow around the box was made of red velvet. Very subtle.

The opening credits began to roll. Kristy whispered slyly, "So who is the special person you're going to share the candy with?"

"Several special people, actually," I whispered back. "If you're at Claudia's on Monday afternoon at five-thirty sharp, you'll find out."

We leaned back and concentrated on popcorn and *Pepperoni Man*. Popcorn and a chiller thriller, I thought, free candy and good friends. What more could I ask for from Valentine's Day?

With a night like this, who needed Ross Brown or a Valentine's Day Dance?

Not me, I thought. Not me.

Dear Reader,

In *Abby's Un-Valentine*, Abby makes it clear that she doesn't like Valentine's Day and doesn't like feeling pressured to celebrate it in a certain way. At the end of the book, Abby spends a very nice Valentine's Day in an unconventional manner — at the movies with Kristy.

Although I love holidays and love celebrating them traditionally, some of the nicest holidays I've spent have been celebrated in an unexpected or nontraditional manner. For several years now, I've spent Thanksgiving with friends in Canada, where Thanksgiving is celebrated earlier in the fall. But my friends prepare a traditional American Thanksgiving dinner, and we always have lots of fun. Then there was last year, when everyone in my family had their own plans for Christmas. But we discovered that my father needed heart surgery in December, so we all changed our plans, and my sister and I ended up spending Christmas with our parents, just like when we were kids. It turned out to be a lovely holiday, and in fact the last Christmas we would spend at the house before my parents decided to sell it.

Holidays are times for celebrating and observing, but you don't have to celebrate traditionally in order to make a holiday special.

Happy reading,

Ann M Martin

Ann M. Martin

About the Author

ANN MATTHEWS MARTIN was born on August 12, 1955. She grew up in Princeton, NJ, with her parents and her younger sister, Jane.

Although Ann used to be a teacher and then an editor of children's books, she's now a full-time writer. She gets ideas for her books from many different places. Some are based on personal experiences. Others are based on childhood memories and feelings. Many are written about contemporary problems or events.

All of Ann's characters, even the members of the Baby-sitters Club, are made up. (So is Stoneybrook.) But many of her characters are based on real people. Sometimes Ann names her characters after people she knows; other times she chooses names she likes.

In addition to the Baby-sitters Club books, Ann Martin has written many other books for children. Her favorite is *Ten Kids, No Pets* because she loves big families and she loves animals. Her favorite Baby-sitters Club book is *Kristy's Big Day*. (By the way, Kristy is her favorite baby-sitter!)

Ann M. Martin now lives in New York with her cats, Gussie, Woody, and Willy. Her hobbies are reading, sewing, and needlework — especially making clothes for children.

Notebook Pages

This Baby-sitters Club book belongs to _____.

I am _____ years old and in the _____

grade.

The name of my school is _____.

I got this BSC book from _____.

I started reading it on _____ and

finished reading it on _____.

The place where I read most of this book is _____.

My favorite part was when _____.

If I could change anything in the story, it might be the part when

_____.

My favorite character in the Baby-sitters Club is _____.

The BSC member I am most like is _____

because _____.

If I could write a Baby-sitters Club book it would be about ____

_____.

#127 Abby's Un-Valentine

In *Abby's Un-Valentine*, Abby makes it perfectly clear that she doesn't like Valentine's Day. I think Valentine's Day is _____ _____. The best Valentine's Day I ever had was when _____

_____

_____. The worst Valentine's Day I ever had was when _____

_____

_____. If I were planning the perfect Valentine's Day, this is what I'd do: _____

_____

_____. Claudia is a big fan of making homemade valentines. If I were making a valentine for one of the BSC members, it would look like this:

ABBY'S

Twins from the start!

My dad could always make me laugh.

SCRAPBOOK

tennis, anyone?

my dad's favorite place.

Look out Hawaii! Here comes the BSC.

Read all the books
about **Abby**
in the Baby-sitters Club series
by Ann M. Martin

Portrait Collection:

Abby's Book
   Abby tells about the tragedies and comedies of her
   up-and-down life.

Look for #128

CLAUDIA AND THE LITTLE LIAR

"Haley," I said, "you stopped Stacey from writing her report, made her go all the way to my house, and then here." My voice rose angrily. "All this time Matt's been waiting for Nicky to bring over the lizard book because he thought I called him. Now it's late. Your parents are going to have to get it when they come in. I don't understand. Why did you do it?"

"You're crazy, Claudia," Haley replied coolly. "I told you Matt needed a book from Nicky and he wanted you to remind him to bring it over."

Haley was really good at this. Her lie was close enough to the truth to give me a moment of doubt. Had I heard her wrong? No. I was sure I hadn't.

Matt tugged at the hem of my shirt. On a card he'd written the name Nicky Pike. I didn't want to let Haley get away, but I had to be fair to Matt. I made a gesture, as if I were talking on the phone, and went to the kitchen to call Nicky. Mrs. Pike answered. She didn't know what book I meant, and Mr. Pike had taken Nicky and the other kids out to a movie. She'd have him call when they returned.

I did my best to explain this to Matt. A look of disappointment swept across his face and I felt terrible. He punched a fist into the palm of his other hand. Although he sometimes has difficulty communicating, at that moment I understood him loud and clear. He was totally frustrated with the confusion of having been misunderstood.

Not exactly misunderstood, though. Haley had understood him perfectly. I was pretty sure of that. She'd just chosen to lie to me again.

THE BABY-SITTERS CLUB®

Collect 'em all!

100 (and more)
Reasons to Stay Friends Forever!

More titles... ▸

The Baby-sitters Club titles continued...

❏ MG22877-3	#93	Mary Anne and the Memory Garden	$3.99
❏ MG22878-1	#94	Stacey McGill, Super Sitter	$3.99
❏ MG22879-X	#95	Kristy + Bart = ?	$3.99
❏ MG22880-3	#96	Abby's Lucky Thirteen	$3.99
❏ MG22881-1	#97	Claudia and the World's Cutest Baby	$3.99
❏ MG22882-X	#98	Dawn and Too Many Sitters	$3.99
❏ MG69205-4	#99	Stacey's Broken Heart	$3.99
❏ MG69206-2	#100	Kristy's Worst Idea	$3.99
❏ MG69207-0	#101	Claudia Kishi, Middle School Dropout	$3.99
❏ MG69208-9	#102	Mary Anne and the Little Princess	$3.99
❏ MG69209-7	#103	Happy Holidays, Jessi	$3.99
❏ MG69210-0	#104	Abby's Twin	$3.99
❏ MG69211-9	#105	Stacey the Math Whiz	$3.99
❏ MG69212-7	#106	Claudia, Queen of the Seventh Grade	$3.99
❏ MG69213-5	#107	Mind Your Own Business, Kristy!	$3.99
❏ MG69214-3	#108	Don't Give Up, Mallory	$3.99
❏ MG69215-1	#109	Mary Anne To the Rescue	$3.99
❏ MG05988-2	#110	Abby the Bad Sport	$3.99
❏ MG05989-0	#111	Stacey's Secret Friend	$3.99
❏ MG05990-4	#112	Kristy and the Sister War	$3.99
❏ MG05911-2	#113	Claudia Makes Up Her Mind	$3.99
❏ MG05911-2	#114	The Secret Life of Mary Anne Spier	$3.99
❏ MG05993-9	#115	Jessi's Big Break	$3.99
❏ MG05994-7	#116	Abby and the Worst Kid Ever	$3.99
❏ MG05995-5	#117	Claudia and the Terrible Truth	$3.99
❏ MG05996-3	#118	Kristy Thomas, Dog Trainer	$3.99
❏ MG05997-1	#119	Stacey's Ex-Boyfriend	$3.99
❏ MG05998-X	#120	Mary Anne and the Playground Fight	$3.99
❏ MG45575-3		Logan's Story Special Edition Readers' Request	$3.25
❏ MG47118-X		Logan Bruno, Boy Baby-sitter Special Edition Readers' Request	$3.50
❏ MG47756-0		Shannon's Story Special Edition	$3.50
❏ MG47686-6		The Baby-sitters Club Guide to Baby-sitting	$3.25
❏ MG47314-X		The Baby-sitters Club Trivia and Puzzle Fun Book	$2.50
❏ MG48400-1		BSC Portrait Collection: Claudia's Book	$3.50
❏ MG22864-1		BSC Portrait Collection: Dawn's Book	$3.50
❏ MG69181-3		BSC Portrait Collection: Kristy's Book	$3.99
❏ MG22865-X		BSC Portrait Collection: Mary Anne's Book	$3.99
❏ MG48399-4		BSC Portrait Collection: Stacey's Book	$3.50
❏ MG92713-2		The Complete Guide to The Baby-sitters Club	$4.95
❏ MG47151-1		The Baby-sitters Club Chain Letter	$14.95
❏ MG48295-5		The Baby-sitters Club Secret Santa	$14.95
❏ MG45074-3		The Baby-sitters Club Notebook	$2.50
❏ MG44783-1		The Baby-sitters Club Postcard Book	$4.95

Available wherever you buy books...or use this order form.

Scholastic Inc., P.O. Box 7502, 2931 E. McCarty Street, Jefferson City, MO 65102

Please send me the books I have checked above. I am enclosing $_____
(please add $2.00 to cover shipping and handling). Send check or money order–
no cash or C.O.D.s please.

Name _____ Birthdate _____

Address _____

City _____ State/Zip _____

BSC1297

THE BABY-SITTERS CLUB

by Ann M. Martin

Collect and read these exciting BSC Super Specials, Mysteries, and Super Mysteries along with your favorite Baby-sitters Club books!

BSC Super Specials

BSC Mysteries

More titles ➡

The Baby-sitters Club books continued...

Available wherever you buy books...or use this order form.

Scholastic Inc., P.O. Box 7502, 2931 East McCarty Street, Jefferson City, MO 65102-7502

Please send me the books I have checked above. I am enclosing $ _____
(please add $2.00 to cover shipping and handling). Send check or money order
— no cash or C.O.D.s please.

Name_____Birthdate_____

Address _____

City_____State/Zip_____

Please allow four to six weeks for delivery. Offer good in the U.S. only. Sorry, mail orders are not
available to residents of Canada. Prices subject to change.   BSCM1297